Beneath Red Tail Wings

Patricia I Williams

Saddleback Legends
A Mythical Legends Publishing Imprint

Beneath Red Tail Wings is a work of fiction. The characters, incidents, and dialogs are products of the author's imagination and are not to be construed as real. Any resemblance to actual events or persons, living or dead, is entirely coincidental.

A Saddleback Legends Mass-Market Paperback Edition

Copyright © 2015 by **Patricia I. Williams**
Mass-Market Paperback published Edition, 2018
Published by Mythical Legends Publishers, 2015
Publisher@mythicallegends.com
http://mythicallegends.com

ISBN-13: 978-1-943958-64-1

Printed in the United States of America
9 8 7 6 5 4 3 2 1

Dedication

Thanks to my Heavenly Father and Jehovah our God.

To those that still ride the range with devotion and to whom that way of life will never die.

Thanks to James, the capo dei capi of publication.

To the cowboys and girls that enthralled me since childhood in history books, in movies and television and fiction.

Beneath Red Tail Wings

6

September 1873 San Francisco, California

Delirium

The festering strips burned, the fever sucked him dry. The voice of his father harangued his ears, accusing.

"Traitorous, wretched boy! No son of mine would do such a thing!"

"How could you do this? Did you think of us, you bastard? Do you know what this means?"

The echo of the door slamming against his battered jaw pounded on his ears until he cried out.

The Captain would hear. He would come and the beatings would begin again.

"Quiet, quiet boy. You want to get caught? You want to the mate to strike with that devilish belayin' pin? You want to lay in the fo'c'sle waiting to die from another beating? You want to run up and down and up and down for days and nights without sleep or vittles? You want to live boy?"

"No no more, no more. Shut up Papa, shut up. You said follow my conscience. You said be a man and make a stand. I made it Papa. I made it.

Ah, don't hate me Papa. Please listen, please!"

"Get out, get out traitorous, wretched boy! Don't show your face again. Traitor!"

He wanted to deny forsaking his family. But the truth could not be denied. They were dead. Father and Royal were dead years gone now, hating him, the traitor. He must keep moving or the Captain would find him. Fearing the tarred ropes and belaying pins striking from the dark, he crawled away from the dock. His body was soaking wet, trembling one moment and burning the next. Desperate, Matthew sucked the briny damp from his filthy shirt. He curled into a stack of cargo already strapped down to be loaded onto another hell ship. He could hear the crowd yelling, demanding the Captain's surrender. He could barely see through his irritated eyes, one swollen shut from a nasty cut and blow to the face he got from a knife or marlinspike. He had never seen it coming.

Charlie had been taken ashore, but the rest of them were not allowed to leave. Lucky Charlie. Say what you want, but he wished he had a friend in this city full of crimps. Benjamin called them that. Crimps. Slave catchers. Need a body? Take it. Matthew was no sailor and tried to explain to the First Mate he was taken under duress. His protest got him a beating. The worst of his life in fact. He had no idea how long he was insensible, but when he was able to stagger from the ragged hammock Harris came and beat him again. Matthew was sure he defended himself the first time, but not this time. There was a belaying pin. He came to, chained to the grates on deck and flogged. It would not be the last time. Mr. Maloney told him to cease resisting and go along so he would stay alive. He was so weak from the beatings and flogging, further protest was impossible anyway.

Months later, Matthew realized it made little difference if he was subservient. He kept his head down and learned to do the work, but feared he would not see land again. Three of the battered crew died. The story was they jumped overboard or fell by accident, but Matthew would always wonder if Harris had outright killed them. Poor John, he was just a boy. Everyone was starving on hardtack and little water. He was shamed he survived because Harris' ire shifted to someone else and they died.

Matthew didn't know if Benjamin put him over the side tonight hoping he would drown or make it out. The man's loyalties shifted each day.

There was some talk about a Sailor's Home for help. Matthew didn't know this place and thought it was a fool's errand. Ben said if he stayed he might just die. He was too weak to fight Ben's insistence. The tide tried to take him away but he grabbed the anchor line and hung on until he got his bearings. The horrific sting of the cold salt water stole his breath. He believed he would drown for sure. How he managed to get onto the pier remained a miracle to him. His nails tore off at the quick from his desperate effort to climb the ladder. The men on the dock were yelling for the Captain's blood, many drunk and angry waving torches and rope for a hanging.

Matthew had enough sense left to scuttle away through stacks of cargo into the shadows between buildings. Rats squealed and ran about in the darkness. He prayed no other crimps found him. Benjamin said if he got caught he would wind up on another ship even broken as he was. Matthew decided he would kill himself for sure to escape another hellish journey like this. His overtaxed body soon failed him. His last thought was he would die in mud reeking of urine and feces.

Rescue

Birds were singing. He must be lying in the four poster with the balcony doors open to catch an errant breeze. Matthew's heart reveled in gratitude. For some reason he was especially glad to hear those chirping ditties that used to drive him mad when he wanted to lie in on school mornings. He was safe now. Somehow all was forgiven and he was home. He waited for his mother to come to him with a cool glass of spring water. Where was she? He was so thirsty.

Father Arturo shook his head in great dismay. Brother Finley worked at his side through the night washing away the filth and cleaning infected wounds across the young man's back and sides. Finley worked with tears in his own eyes until sent away to sleep. In four hours they would trade places beside the cot in the ongoing effort to save this poor soul found in an filthy alley just off the waterfront.

When conscious, the man struggled against the bindings that kept him on his stomach. His back was exposed to the air, the flesh extremely raw from the lancing of the wounds and the harsh carbolic acid wash. The priest hoped he would not be reduced to begging honey or vinegar to keep the wounds clean of further infection.

He was grateful a recent graduate of Tolands Medical College had dared to set up practice nearby. The young English doctor was brimming with enthusiasm and new ideas, but had a razor sharp tongue. That was evident when they were all flayed for washing the wounds out with the carbolic, which was supposed to be used to clean the room! Father Arturo feared the realities of life the seamen endured would crush the young man's idealism and fervor.

There was certainly little money to support a practice. The doctor would probably leave for a more prosperous part of town and perhaps do charitable work out of St. Mary's. For now Father Arturo would be grateful to God for His mercy and timely intervention that this life may be saved.

Collapsing onto the stool, Arturo's prayers gave way to the meditative stanzas of the Rosary through which he asked the Blessed Mother to pray for the boy's deliverance. Jesus would surely see to it he roused if the poor soul took a turn for the worse. The exhausted man ignored the racket from the street. The humid air was not very good for a sick soul, heavy with foul odors as it was. But leaving the boy to breath air thick with sick and blood could not be good either. So they left the shutters ajar.

Shouting men carried on with the labor of the day. Harness jangled, horses and mules whinnied and brayed. The high pitched voices of children piped up hawking the home grown vegetables for their mothers. The meager goods were spread out on blankets in the street. The less fortunate children handed out advertising bills from more nefarious employers. Occasionally the sounds would escalate, fueled by arguments and the crack of whips. When the day began to wane, hysterical laughter and screams would add to the chaotic music from the saloons and cribs several blocks away. These dens of iniquity enticed the day laborers to throw away their pitiful earnings on drink and fornication. They were a small part of the overwhelming number that infested the city like fleas.

The priest's efforts to turn men from this folly had not been fruitful. Father Arturo labored against a rising tide of sin from the clapboard structure his group moved into. After driving out the rats and roaches, they offered reasonably clean cots and what medicine they had available from donations. Sometimes medicine was what they stirred up in the kitchen. There were a few men who turned up for confession, weeping over their inability to fight the addiction to liquor and opium. Prayers were said, comfort given and the cycle would begin again. By the Grace of God he escaped many promised beatings from the owner of the local establishments. The sailors and freight drivers threatened to burn the saloon down if hands were laid on a priest or the lay brothers who offered them succor. Sometimes that care was only reasonably clean water and rags to wash away blood, before these men waded back into the cesspit that was their daily life.

Father Arturo dipped the chair back against the gray wall to rest his aching head. Brother Finley woke him up at dawn. The lay brother was upset about resting all night while the priest remained on watch. Arturo listened, mildly amused, to the tirade as he checked on their sleeping patient once more.

The Pit of Despair

The days faded into one another, a sad parade with tired men struggling to save a soul with no desire left to survive. When conscious the poor boy stared as if horror struck for endless hours. His voice was lost completely after screaming, crying and begging through relentless nightmares. Their touch, their very presence finally became unremarked. Exhaustion forced his eyes to shut but when awake, only the stare. The doctor declared his mind was possibly broken forever. But Father Arturo would not give up. They forced broth into the unresisting husk at every opportunity, continued to treat his wounds and prayed.

Four months later Matthew made the effort to stand on his own two legs. He did not know if he was grateful to these men who labored so hard to save him. Two thick limbs from a tree were held in shaky fists propping him up. He remained plagued by bouts of dizziness and his vision seem to be impaired for the long haul. Sometimes the battered muscles in his thighs and legs cramped so tightly he feared they would tear loose from his bones. Dr. Everley assured him that time would resolve these issues, but Matthew worried he was going blind as some days his vision appeared worse than others. Assurances meant nothing to him at this point. He'd been blind before.

His recovery was tedious, the depression worse than any he suffered during the war. Fear was a specter which hovered over his shoulders. What if Harris or the Captain found out he was here and not dead overboard? What if someone carried the tale? He knew from the priest there had been searches carried out. Accusations of bribery, outright lies and speculation had fueled gossip and many outright fights in the street outside their doors. He avoided reading about the searches and the trial of the Sunrise. For the first time in his life Matthew was unsure he could stand up for what was right. The desire to flee was all there was left of him. Even after Father Arturo declared the monstrous duo incarcerated, fear dogged his waking and sleeping hours.

His letter to McNamara had gone unanswered so far. Therein he confided in his law partner about the attack and his subsequent travail at sea. Expressing his desire to be shut of the city and Harris, Matthew wished only to be gone and rebuild his life. The priest had sent an accompanying letter stating how he had found Matthew and the months of recovery. Matthew

truly hoped he could be smuggled out of the city
without Harris finding out. He was plagued by
nightmares of the man. He would awaken choking
on bile and gagging and sometimes crying aloud.
It shamed him to be in such a state.

Why had he survived the war against his
kin and the Indians only to come to this? Was it
punishment for taking the stand which betrayed
his family and way of life? Was God truly seeing
him as a turncoat? Would he ever see his way
clear of guilt and punishment? All he had left
was a thorough disillusionment with life and
the conviction one day he would be even more
helpless when the periodic blindness was a
permanent state. Even if he could remain in law
for now, how could he go before a jury or make a
living once blind?

Morning arrived after another sleepless night.
Matthew eased into an old pea coat and made his
way out the back door of the derelict storefront.
He grimaced at the pull of scar tissue on his back.
He wished to forget the horrible experience of the
brothers forcing him to move about so the worst
of the scars would not cripple him.

The priest and his assistants barely managed
to get by in their efforts to minister to the riff raff
that populated this area off the waterfront.

Matthew didn't even know where they were in the city. He never asked. What did it matter?

He eased down upon an old crate and let the weak sun attempt to warm his exhausted body. The yard was muddy with only a rope strung between the building and a pole for the endless washing. The ragged bedding stirred in the chill breeze. Matthew realized some of the stains that would not wash away were caused by his own blood. Everything was washed and scrubbed and used again. The brother's hands were raw and calloused from their constant labor and scalding water. No one gave a damn, not about them and not about him. No one. He ignored the big barrel of water boiling, full of rags and sheets even now. It added little warmth to combat the foggy atmosphere.

As fast as the public appeared enraged by the torture of the crew, the winds had changed and Captain Clarke was once again being hailed as a bastion of good will. If Matthew ever got the chance, he would kill Clarke. He wanted Harris dead too, so very much. But the thought of that brute set him to trembling and tearing up like a baby. When nightmares plagued him, Matthew had thrown himself against the walls of his room in terror. He learned his lessons well, the size of a man doesn't give you any idea of how much of a monster he could be. Matthew promised himself, he would get better with a gun. He would never be taken again.

Distractions

Father Arturo entertained Matthew with stories of his personal travels from Spain to Rome, where he studied for the priesthood. His family was well off and expected him to rise to power in the church. But God had other plans for Arturo. Waylaid by robbers during his travels, a poor man rescued him even though his family were suffering lean times. Arturo never forgot that selfless kindness. His father settled no little gold on the man for the sparing of his son. Later Arturo's father was not so overjoyed when that same son took vows to minister to the diseased and desperate. So instead of treading the golden halls of the Vatican, Arturo crossed the world to find his calling among the miserable souls that ferried the world's wealth in the great sailing vessels.

As the months passed, Matthew's spirit was soothed by the unrelenting faith the brothers expressed as they labored and the sameness of his days. Their kindness never wavered even as their patience was tested to its limits. He occupied himself in a relentless focus on weaving bits of string and rope into Solomon knots. He wore the bracelets he made or left them lying around the place for the errant sailor to pick up. Some days he blocked out his surroundings completely in a desperate effort not to remember his experiences. No war, no ship, no Harris.

When he was not intent on the one thing he learned on the hell ship, Matthew helped the brothers do their work around the place. Soon his own hands were raw from the endless chore of washing sheets and boiling bandages. He hammered nails into ill-fitting planks to patch the leaking roof and cover gaps which let in chilled air. Some days he would sweep the floors and Father Arturo would warn the brothers off while Matthew completed turn after turn through the sanctuary, his mind lost to the movement of broom back and forth. As suddenly as he became lost in repetitive actions, Matt would be reconnecting with everyone again, listening to their stories and absorbed in Arturo's history lessons.

Time lost all meaning to the healing man. Matthew considered remaining inside the confines of the Father's mission forever. He was safe there, hiding from a world filled with enemies wanting his demise.

1877 Colorado Rockies

Discovery

Matt dangled from the end of the rope, his chest scrapping against the side of the cliff. He would have more than a few abrasions after this was done. Sweat from exertion and the sun baked rocks stung his eyes. He was pretty much climbing blind, depending on his pony to get them up. The man hitched to his back was shorter than he, but at least twenty to thirty pounds heavier. That he was unconscious added to the problem of getting him back up to the narrow trail. Blood from a bullet wound in the man's shoulder soaked the back of Matt's shirt.

He braced his legs once more and pulled himself up another foot. His old pony continued to take up the slack, holding steady against all the cropped eared evidence suggesting he was a killer to anyone fool enough to mount up. Matt's gloved hands scrabbled for a hold onto the crumbling edge of the drop off. He was suddenly dragged over the top a few feet more before Cobby snorted in relief and returned to nipping at the sparse grass. He lay for a moment gasping for breath, the man a dead weight on top of him.

After a minute or two, Matt squirmed out from under the body. He got his canteen from Cobby's saddle and used a little to moisten the man's parched lips. The bullet had passed through the body so Matt poured a little of his last few swallows of whiskey in the holes then used his one clean bandana and a few strips of rawhide to tie down for a bandage. The man had lost a lot of blood and his face was pale and sweaty with shock. Now they were up here, Matt hoped that the darkening sky wouldn't bring a storm before he found some place to hold up with his unconscious charge.

Cobby snorted and pranced away as Matt pulled him over to the body. His legs were no longer trembling from the climb, so he figured he could hoist the man into the saddle and get moving. The old pony's notched ears were flat and teeth bared. But he stood perfectly still under the weight and didn't kick Matt in the head as he tied the man's wrists to the saddle before mounting up behind him. There wasn't any sign of a horse running down the trail ahead of him, so Matt wondered where the man's horse could have gone. Thunder rumbled in the distance. He knew a night in the rain would probably end the man.

They journeyed for maybe an hour before the first icy drops fell. Matt covered the man with his slicker and put his own wool lined jacket and gloves on. The temperature dropped abruptly. If he had to make do with the sparse trees they would both probably get struck by lightning. Thunder echoed around the mountains and Cobby threw up his head and refused to move another inch.

"Come on you mule headed nag. You won't stay dry standing around out here."

Dismounting, Matt grabbed the bridle and halter alongside Cobby's jaw and pulled him along the narrow trail he had been following. The old horse kept baring his teeth and snorting all the while but didn't kick or bite. The trail was too wide to be an animal track, so perhaps there was a cave or cabin at the end of it. At this point a cave would be grand as long as it was free of bears.

Lightning cracked overhead, scaring the hell out of man and horse. Some distance away a tree sizzled as it burst into flames, but the sudden torrent of rain thankfully overwhelmed the fire. The first flash of light left the impression of some kind of structure ahead. Relief was quickly replaced by caution. Whoever ambushed the old man could be hold up there. For the first time in months, Matt pulled his gun.

He took time scouting the area thoroughly before approaching the building. Just because he didn't see any lights didn't mean a killer couldn't be watching from the dark windows. Someone wanted this man dead. They could still be around. It wouldn't be the first time and the thought of that incident made him shiver. His mother used to say someone was stepping on your grave when that feeling crawled up your spine. So he made himself wait until his nerves settled before he circled the cabin and eased along the west wall to the door.

He nudged the door open with his gun barrel. Rusty hinges resisted the intrusion, but the door swung back against the wall. He eased down and went in low, the pounding rain covering his first cautious entry. Lightning lit up the night and the sudden flare exposed no other intruders, though it was a near thing not to fire his weapon at the shadows! Matt holstered his gun. He had the impression of a table with a lamp atop it. He hoped there was oil. A crude fireplace was the last image from the lightning flash. It would do. So he hurried out to bring the wounded man in.

First he carried the old man inside and laid him on the floor nearest the fireplace. Matt stripped the saddle and his meager supplies from the pony. He hobbled old Cobby in the wind protected space between the cabin and the rock wall that rose up behind it. He hoped the battered overhang resembling a back porch would be enough shelter from the lightning. Matt wanted to take him inside the cabin, but Cobby hated barns, stalls and men in general. He tied on the feed bag with the last of the oats he'd bought in Silverton. He left the horse rolling his eyes and staring him down with laid back notched ears. There would be hell to pay come morning for leaving him out here, but having a right fit thrown inside and stomping on his patient wouldn't do.

Matt felt his way to the fireplace, finding fairly dry kindling already laid and a rusted crane and trivet. He took flint and steel from the inside pocket of his coat and set to work. He was relieved when smoke disappeared up the chimney and the tiny flame grew. Thank goodness there was wood already stacked against the wall. He was dogged tired and still needed to bed down his feverish patient.

Matt removed the man's outer garments and boots. He discovered a crude bunk and took the dusty blankets for a good shake in the open doorway. He dragged the bunk over to the fire, then lifted the old man atop it, tucking him in against the damp. A further search of the single room turned up kerosene and a few cans of beans and peaches. Someone obviously used the place from time to time. The cans weren't old and the blankets weren't moth eaten. He filled the lamp and lit it. Unpacking his gear, Matt got coffee going with collected rainwater. After checking the shutters were secure, he latched the door. When the room warmed up he shucked off his coat and hat. After a while the scent of frying bacon and potatoes filled the room.

He checked the old man's wound, cleaning the holes out by lamp light. All that time lying in the open and then the ride just might do him in. Matt hadn't heard any shots the last days riding in the mountains. He would have thought the sound would have carried to him. The fact that a fat roll of bank notes and silver dollars remained in the money belt around his waist, was a sure indication of why the old man was bushwhacked. But Matt couldn't just leave him. Nobody should have to die alone.

Exhausted, Matt finally set down to the unsteady table to eat. The crude chair rocked on its uneven legs until he sat in it. A can of beans and peaches bulked up his meal. Those rare peach slices were much appreciated. There wasn't any money left for pleasures like these right now. The bread, cheese and the rest of his meager stores would have to be rationed until he could get out of this situation. Matt needed to get a job before his last few dollars were gone. He wasn't always welcome at smaller homesteads, because of his worn clothes and nightmare pony. He usually worked the ranches as he traveled, but steered clear of the mining operations. The rowdy mining camps were filled with rotgut and greedy men scrabbling over silver and the few women that dared to try and survive there. A law abiding man had to keep close watch on his property and worry too much about a bullet in the back. Those places brought back bad memories.

Luck graced him once more when he discovered a thick bar of wood leaning in a dark corner of the room which he used to keep the door firmly shut. The latch was no more than tattered rope over a nail. Now there would be warning if those bushwhackers showed up. He built up the fire considerably before he bedded down on the floor, hopefully to get a full night's sleep without dreams. Mindful of that money belt, he tucked it in next to the man. He didn't need to be accused of theft. The old man had been shot from the front. He wasn't wearing a gun. The horse and rifle he should have had was gone without a trace. Matt slept with his rifle close at hand by the fireplace. Contrary as ever, dreams did not disturb his rest at all during the remainder of the stormy night.

The rain pummeled the cabin for three days. Random holes in the roof left puddles on the floor. Matt had to move his bedroll twice to avoid the irritating splashes of cold water startling him from sleep. The old man's fever worsened and for a while Matt was sure he wouldn't make it, but he was a tough one alright. For the time being his fever was down and his breathing deep. Maybe he would wake up soon and tell Matt where he should take him. Right now his most dangerous task was seeing to his right irritated pony. No, Matt didn't shiver as he cautiously made his way across the muddy track to the back of the cabin.

Intruders Welcomed

Cobby was staring at him with white rimmed eyes and teeth bared in righteous indignation. The wall eyed grulla's hide gleamed in the sun from an intensive currying. His stubby tail and scant mane were free of tangles and burrs. Matt wiped the sweat from his face with his forearm. He surveyed the result of his labor with a faint smile. Cobby was hobbled for the moment, otherwise he would be trying his best to kick in Matt's ribs. Pulling that rawhide loose was going to be an adventure.

The cowboy smiled as he ran toward the cabin, dodging the snake like lunge of the ewe necked devil. He wiped his boots along the porch edge before he went into the cabin.

He checked his patient, still resting quietly. Matt was pretty confident whoever tried to rob the old man had given up. The weather should have further discouraged them. It must have been a pretty cowardly bunch, since the money wasn't taken. He had met few men in this country not tough enough to climb down there and take what they killed for.

Matt foraged some wild greens and snared a couple of rabbits on his fifth day. The old man had swallowed some of the broth off the meager stew Matt had boiled up and kept on the fire. Now there was more confidence the man would recover. Matt settled down to eat, grimacing at the lack of salt and seasoning, but grateful all the same to not have an empty belly.

After cleaning up he stepped outside again leaning against the wall to roll a smoke. It wasn't a regular habit, but he was bored. There weren't any old magazines or newspapers in the cabin and Cloth of Gold was memorized from constant use. Sooner or later he would get back to Silverton or Denver and get some new reading material. Maybe he would winter up here in this cabin. With a little patch work it could be secure. Even with the signs of regular use, he would hope who ever laid up wintered someplace else. He never liked staying over in Denver for the winters. But logic demanded he learn more about surviving the weather before taking the chance on living alone during snow season.

Matt was taking his last drag on the butt, when Cobby's head swung up, ears pricked forward. He turned to face the trail they had come in on. A horse whinnied, not close by yet. Matt reached inside the door and picked up his rifle, stepping back into the dim room. Cobby snorted and backed up near the cabin wall, nostrils flared and teeth bared in antagonistic greeting.

Three riders emerged from the stand of aspen around the cabin. A boney shouldered old man lead the procession, his eyes lost in wrinkles and weathered face. A white handlebar mustache dropped over his thin lips, tainted yellow from tobacco. There was a girl riding behind him with copper hair, shot through with gold and red sparks from the sunlight. Another man rode up beside the girl. He took off his hat and shook the water off it, then mopped his face with a handkerchief. He leaned toward the girl and said something to her. Her chin went up and she shook her head, stubborn refusal obvious on her face. He flushed pink and jerked his horses' reins hard, riding up next to the old man. His blond hair was cut close in the eastern way, thick and curling with pomade. Even from inside the cabin Matt could see the vivid blue of his eyes.

"Hallo the house," the old man called. "We smelled the smoke. We're lookin' fer someone."

Matt stepped out onto the porch, his rifle held casually in both hands.

"You're not looking for me mister. I don't know you," he growled.

He saw the men straighten in their saddles,

suddenly wary.

"Now wait a minute son, don't get testy. My names Gil Jones, foreman of the Rocking Falls Ranch on the plain below these here mountains. We're lookin' for the boss man Will Bethencourt."

"He's my father. I'm Sarah Bethencourt. Please have you seen any strangers or heard anything? He's been missing near a week."

Sarah moved her horse ahead of her companions, ignoring Gil's upraised hands to warn her back.

"Please sir, have you seen anyone? How long have you been here?"

"Hold on a minute lady. How do I know you're really who you say you are? A pretty face don't mean you can't be up to no good."

"Wait just a minute. Who the hell...," the blond put his hand on the butt of his sidearm and Matt's rifle shifted, aimed dead center.

"Stop it Kevin. The man is right. He doesn't know who we are. Here, look here."

Sarah reached inside the collar of her shirt and pulled out a locket dangling from a silver chain. She lifted it over her head, anxious hands fumbling her first attempts to get it untangled from the long copper braid.

"Here, look inside. There's a picture of my

father, mother and I."

"Toss it over here," Matt demanded.

He caught the locket out of the air with his left hand and stepped back inside the cabin. He recognized the man as the same one lying in the bunk behind him. The hair was darker, but the cut and heavy mustache was the same. Sarah was a little girl posing between him and a thin fragile looking woman. Obviously Sarah took after the woman in looks. Matt closed the locket and stepped outside.

"Miss Bethencourt, your father's inside."

"Thank you!" Sarah quickly shifted to dismount.

"Hold on, hold on. He's been hurt and still unconscious!"

She was already pushing passed him while he was speaking. He heard her worried cry and then she was calling Gil to come to her.

Matt stepped aside as the two men stepped down from their horses and rushed the cabin. He followed, rifle trained on their backs. While the trio hovered over the bunk, Matt pushed the shutter back letting in more light and waited for their next move.

"That's a bullet wound Miss Sarah and looks like he's been bashed about the head too."

While Gil and Sarah were examining the wounds and black bruises, the one called Kevin turned to Matt, his hand once more sliding to his holstered gun.

"Mister, Mr. Bethencourt was carrying a lot of money, just where did you say ..."

"I didn't say," snapped Matt. "Whatever he had on him is still on him. I'm no thief."

"Kevin! Dad's money belt is right here."

"What?"

The blond's face was blank with shock. He stared at Matt in disbelief, his face once again rosy.

"Well damn mister. I don't know what to say. I'd like you to accept my apologies. It's been such a worrisome time. We've been just at the end of our rope."

He took off his gloves and offered Matt his hand. His smile was disarming. Matt looked him in the eyes and saw nothing but a rather embarrassed younger man trying to impress a girl. He shook the proffered hand. Kevin sighed in relief and couldn't stop the side long glance in Sarah's direction.

'No harm done, Mr. ...?"

"Oh, Harlan. Kevin Harlan. I really am sorry for my crude accusations."

"Apology accepted Mr. Harlan, though you aught to know accusations like that can get you shot out here. My name is Matthew Travers."

"Really pleased to meet you, Matthew. It's a good thing you came along when you did. Sarah was out of her mind with worry."

"Glad I could help."

Matt sat his rifle down and motioned Kevin to the table.

"Take a load off. Coffee's hot."

"Good I could use a cup." Kevin sat down and poured the thick black concoction that Matt called coffee. He couldn't stop the grimace at the bitter taste, however.

"Sorry about that. You might want to water that down some."

Kevin grinned and his face got all rosy again.

"Well it is rather strong." He laughed then and gratefully took the canteen Matt was offering to pour some water in his cup. Matt was rather embarrassed himself. He wasn't much of a cook.

Sarah finally moved away from her father's side and approached the table.

"Thank you Mr. Travers, thank you so much. I'm sending Gil for the rest of the men. One of them can ride for the doctor."

"There's a doctor around here?"

"There's a doctor out at the Wimbly Ranch. Some cousin of theirs from Silverton," Kevin interjected.

"He came to assist their cook. She's having a baby and always has trouble. I hope he's still there."

"Well there's not much grub left. I got some rabbit and wild greens in that pot on the fire. And there's cans of beans and peaches."

"That's alright Mr. Travers. I'm sure we can add to it." Sarah gave her father's savior a smile.

"You men sit and have your coffee. I'll take care of the horses," Matt offered.

"Thanks Matt, but Gil's the one needing rest. Old bones, you know."

Kevin laughed and followed Sarah outside. He didn't see the look of disgust that twisted Gil's face.

"Young upstart," Gil grumbled. "Thinks he knows it all."

Matt hid his amusement as Gil got up and stumped out to take care of his own horse. Sarah rushed back in and began unloading the saddlebags she dumped on the table.

"We'll just heat these up," she said laying aside a bundle.

"They're biscuits," she grinned at Matt, "and

you can drop this into the pot with your rabbit."

She tossed Matt another bundle which turned out to be half a cooked rabbit.

"I've also got some cheese and bacon. There is a little bit of flour and salt too."

Matt dropped the rabbit into his pot and added the little sack of salt.

"I have a few snares out since morning. I should go check them. A couple more rabbits wouldn't hurt nothing."

"Alright Mr. Travers. When you get back supper should be ready. Oh, Mr. Travers?"

"Matt will do mam."

"Ah yes. Well Matt, thank you again for saving my father."

"It was purely an accident mam. I'd been tracking this hawk's flight and just happen to look down and see your father lying on this ledge. I wasn't sure if he was alive, so I climbed down. It's a good thing Cobby's such a good cow pony. I'd never got him up otherwise."

"My father had fallen off a cliff!" Sarah's face paled during Matt's description of her father's rescue.

"Sorry mam. I didn't mean to scare you. It was about an hour back that away."

Matt pointed to the east and Sarah paled even

more. She sat down and Matt quickly pour her a cup of coffee.

"Here Miss drink this. I didn't mean to cause you more upset."

"What's going on in here? Sarah are you alright?"

Kevin's voice startled Matt so, he almost reached for his sidearm, which was still lying on his bedroll. He stepped away from the table to cover the move. Trust some girl with eyes the color of new pennies to make him forget he was surrounded by strangers. He turned to face Kevin and spoke more sharply than he intended.

"I thought she was fainting."

"Father had fallen off a cliff!"

"What? Sarah honey, you're white as a sheet."

He hurried to her side and took her into his arms, murmuring whatever nonsense women wanted to hear when upset.

"Leave us alone a minute, will you. You didn't have to tell any horror stories." Kevin was frowning at Matt over Sarah's shoulder.

Sarah tried to object but Kevin's arms tightened more pressing her face into his neck. It was Matt's turn to stump outdoors. He snatched his coat off the nail by the door and was gone into the trees. Kevin shushed Sarah's protests and continued to rub her shoulders. Soon he was kissing her forehead and cheeks. He kissed her lips, deepening the kiss fairly quickly. Sarah began to struggle.

Kevin, my father and the door's open. What are you doing, stop it!"

She pushed him away.

"God Sarah, I'm sorry. You just go to my head. You're so beautiful. Every time I hold you. I'm sorry, really." He grinned sheepishly and backed away from her.

"Forgive me? Please?"

She was frowning and it took a heartbeat longer than normal for her to give him a shaky smile. He was peeking at her from under long pale lashes, his eyes imploring.

"Alright Kevin. I didn't mean to snap."

"I know honey. You're tired and I'm being a bore. Here sit down and drink your coffee. I'll get the rest of our things. Once the doctor gets here and your father's home you'll feel better."

Sarah watched him go outside. Then turned her thoughts to putting together a meal.

Speculations and Aggravations

Mr. Travers surprised them all leaving her father's money on him like that. His frayed store bought clothes and that horrible looking animal they saw near the cabin marked him as a very poor man. Most cowboys were working for a dollar a day. Sarah wondered if the long scar on his cheek was gotten in a knife fight. The oddest thing was the spectacles he wore. The lenses were smokey gray and seemed to wrap around the sides. She had yet to see his eyes, but he didn't appear to be short sighted, certainly not when holding them off with that rifle.

Contrary to most cowhand habits, his guns were well oiled and clean. He moved quiet too. For all the inconsistencies his integrity was obvious. He looked directly at everyone he spoke to, catching their eyes. Sarah's father always remarked on men who wouldn't or couldn't. She tried to think what color they could be behind those gray lenses. His skin was tanned and his hair was deep brown, near black. It was shaggy and curled around his ears and shoulders. It was a mess but he obviously made regular use of a straight razor.

She had no fondness for beards, although her father favored them. He used to tease her by giving her bushy kisses. She would squeal and make a break from fiery cheeks rubbed red by the wiry hair. She loved her father but his ideas of affection usually left her feeling more than ever, she should have been a boy.

Sarah placed the sliced cheese on the table and supplemented Matt's dented plates with their utensils. They could eat soon as the biscuits were warmed through. Sarah raked the hot ashes over her tightly wrapped treasures and stepped outside. She was standing under lowering skies when Matt returned. She never heard his passage through the woods. He glanced her way but went inside. She should go in and dish up his food. Her father would surely give the man a job after all he'd done for him. When Sarah got inside Matt was hunched down by the fire eating from his battered plate. Two skinned rabbits hung from a hook off the mantle. Kevin and Gil came in behind her heading straight for the freshened coffee. She quickly dished up the stew for the other men and turned out the biscuits. Making her own plate Sarah sat down in the wobbly chair at the table. She passed the plate of cheese to each man. Matt got up and opened two cans of peaches and passed it around.

"I have to make sure to come back up here and replace what I used. Somebody obviously stops off here from time to time."

"Might not be friendlies. Kind of off the usual trails," Gil commented.

"Yeah I did wonder on that. Was only luck I found it in that thunderstorm. Almost passed it by. It would have been bad for both of us with the lightning and all."

"Yep, Mr. Bethencourt was lucky you came along. We might have never found him. How did you manage that anyway?" Kevin looked curiously at Matt.

"I noticed a couple of red tails seem to be keeping to my trail. I was looking for their nest when I noticed him. Didn't see any sign of his horse though. Thought that odd, but didn't have time to look around. The storm moved in real fast and the lightning got bad. Even after the rain stopped I couldn't see trying to take him anywhere in his condition. He seems to be resting better. We should all turn in early tonight anyway. It looks like another storm maybe brewing."

"I'll go along with that suggestion young feller. I'm plum tuckered myself. If I'm gonna ride down the mountain I'll need to start out at dawn to get to our base camp. Hope you're wrong about that storm though. It could last another couple a days and Will needs that sawbones."

There wasn't much said after that. The group addressed their hungry middles and didn't leave any left overs. Matt put the rabbits on a spit to roast before he spread his bedroll on the floor.

Sarah looked beyond him to see her bedroll setting atop her saddle by the bunk. Gil rolled his blankets out on the other side of the fireplace and was soon covered up with his hat over his face. Matt followed suit leaving his rifle propped against the fireplace at his shoulder, his gun holstered on his hip because there were strangers all around him now. Kevin and Sarah looked at each other and shrugged. In a few minutes they were all lying down. Kevin positioning himself beside her.

Matt lay awake a long time under the cover of his hat listening to the rustles and sighs as everyone settled. He hoped the man could travel in a few more days anyway. It was good there were folks looking for him and could take over. But it was still nerve wracking to be around people he didn't know.

It seemed like minutes later Matt opened his eyes to watch Gil tiptoe out into the dawn's light. Kevin rolled out of his blankets with a groan and stumbled out the door behind him. After a while Matt stirred and stoked up the fire, putting on the coffee. He took a can of beans, heated them in the skillet and tossed in the last two biscuits. He went to the door calling out to Gil, startling both men.

"There's bean and biscuits on the table for you. I'm thinking you got a long ride and its real cold this morning."

Gil strode into the cabin peering up into Matt's face. He grinned and patted the younger man's arm.

"Thank ye kindly son. It's pretty nippy and a full belly will help me along."

With that he sat and wolfed down everything in a few minutes. He drank two cups of coffee before putting on his coat. Sarah set up at that moment yawning and stretching.

"Oh Gil why'd you let me sleep so long. You need breakfast at least."

"It's alright Miss Sarah, Matt here rustled me up some grub and stuffed me right good. I'm on my way."

He walked over to the bunk and kissed Sarah on the forehead.

"Don't you worry yourself honey. I'll be back with the boys to get Will home and the doc should meet us there."

Sarah smiled and hugged his neck.

"I don't know what Father and I would ever do without you Uncle Gil. I love you."

"Girl don't start all that mush. Let me out a here boys. I'll be bawling like a dogie in a minute." Gil laughed and stepped out. Kevin called after him.

"You be careful ole man. Whoever waylaid Mr. Bethencourt might still be around!"

"Only if they want a belly full a lead." Gill called back slapping his sidearm. He stepped into the saddle and turned his chestnut cow pony into the trees.

Sarah cooked breakfast and spent the remainder of the morning tending her father. Kevin was talkative, however she noticed Matt spoke very little. After seeing to his horse, he ate with them but retreated to the doorway to read. He put on those odd four lens spectacles when the sky cleared and sparkling sunlight filtered through the trees.

"How long have you been reading that book Matt?" Kevin asked. The blond was leaning forward in the chair squinting at the dog eared yellowing pages. "What's it about?"

"It's called Cloth of Gold, Henry Aldrich. It's a book of poetry."

"Aldrich, Aldrich. Hey that the same fellow who wrote A Story of a Bad Boy?"

Matt looked up and nodded. "The very same. I never read that one. Got this in a dry goods store in Denver a few years back. The clerk tossed it in my kit. Said he was done with it."

"And you still reading it after all this time? You really must like poetry." He rocked the chair in his amusement.

"I do." Matt returned to his reading.

"No offense Matt. It's just you don't look like a poetry reader to me."

"Kevin."

"Ah, Sarah I was just kidding around."

"It's fine Miss Bethencourt. Reading material is hard to find in this country. Poetry was a gift of sorts."

"What do you mean?"

"Friend of mine in the war had an interest in poetry. When he got killed, I got his belongings. He had no family to speak of so I kept his written efforts. I planned to have them published one day, but..."

Matt's expression darkened. He frowned and returned the book to his saddlebags.

"Pardon me mam."

He picked up his hat from the saddle on the floor and stepped out the door.

"Wait Matt. I'm sorry. We didn't..."

"Ah Sarah, let him go. We didn't do anything. Probably just bad memories."

"We should apologize. It wasn't right for us to

pry."

"We didn't pry. You asked a question and he answered. He could have begged off. He'll get over it. Don't get so worked up."

"I don't want him to leave angry Kevin. We owe the man."

"Well honey, why don't you give him some money now and send him on his way."

"We can't do that. He saved father's life. Father would want to meet the man that risked his own to save him."

"Maybe so, but I still think you should pay the man and let him go about his business. Gil and the boys will be back soon enough. Beside's we don't know anything about him. Maybe us showing up disrupted his plans."

"Plans? What possible plans could he make? He could have left father to die and stolen the money. We would never have known. Instead he treated his wounds and stayed with him."

"Maybe someone else got to Mr. Bethencourt before him. It would be easy to save him and then cash in later. It's no secret in the territory your father is well off. Between the Army contracts and his interest in the silver mines, he's worth ten times what's in that belt."

"Kevin, this is ridiculous! There's no logic..."

"Ridiculous, we've only got his word he pulled your father off a ledge!"

"I won't listen to this nonsense."

Kevin left the chair and grabbed Sarah by the shoulders.

"Let go of me. How dare you!"

"Sarah, Sarah damn it! Calm down. I'm just asking you to think! Stop it girl. Your father's life's at stake!"

Sarah gasped and stopped pushing at Kevin to stare at him.

"Sarah honey, I'm not saying not to be grateful. I'm just saying be careful. Don't let gratitude blind you to what's possible. We don't know this man and he could have plans. We have to protect your father until he can take care of himself. I may be paranoid, but better safe than sorry."

"I'm, I'm sorry. You're right. I guess I've been so happy I didn't want to think the worst thing..."

"It's okay Sarah." Kevin said, pulling Sarah into this chest and stroking her hair. She rested against his shoulder. He caressed her until the shivers ceased. Finally he stepped back and looked into her face.

"You still mad?"

She had the grace to blush scarlet.

"No, I'm sorry Kevin. I misjudged you. I thought you were...well, never mind forget it. I need to consider what you said. Help me Kevin, help me keep an eye on Mr. Travers."

Kevin gave Sarah his most dazzling smile and hugged her again.

"You bet honey. Don't worry I'm staying right by your side."

She hugged him tightly and sighed when he buried his face into her hair. Sometimes Kevin was so gallant and other times she wanted to hit him over the head with a pan. Now was not one of those times. He had a point. Matt Travers was a stranger. Maybe only what he appeared to be, a good man in a country where law abiding were few. But to protect her father she could not let her softer emotions interfere with caution. If the man did not look so...ah well, enough of such thoughts. Her father came first. Travers could take care of himself.

Torments of the Mind

Matt took deep breaths of the rain washed air, cleansing his mind of dark memories. The battlefields and his punishment aboard the Sunrise cursed his rest even after these many years. He had met other men broken by the war, wandering aimless, sometimes so damaged they were helpless to do more than drink or drug themselves to death.

He could still see his mother's face, stern and resolute, when he returned home. Father had already acquired the regulation uniforms, a pale gray almost white outfit with scarlet trimmings. He was busy organizing his overseers and servants to manage while he was away. Benjamin, his wife and children had just arrived from their home in Georgia. Their youngest brother Leo, at sixteen, would be left behind to care for the women. Matt had feared the coming confrontation that was to leave him further outcast and he was not wrong. His father was struck speechless, then shut himself away in his office. Benjamin had responded with fists, until the women intervened. His mother, shaking with tearful frustration, showed him the door. She berated him in French, the language rarely spoken around the plantation since his grandmere had passed.

"What foolishness. The disgrace. How can you defy family over something like this? How could you think of pointing a gun at your father or your brother? No son of mine could do this!"

But he stood his ground, followed his principles and plunged into a hell. He lost that naive belief that blood honorably sacrificed would cure the country's ills. He discovered Northern sympathizers usually had as much disdain for his views in regards to the Negro question as his family. Every bullet fired may have struck his loved ones. He fought at Antietam, surprised to survive with painful but quickly healing wounds. The lack of effective leadership in the Union army appalled him. Men died by the hundreds, by the thousands.

Matt returned home after the conflict relieved to discover the house intact at least. All around was evidence that the war had encroached onto home ground. Pits from shelling covered a field that had always been filled with tobacco. Poorly marked graves were the only thing planted there now. Graves even edged one of the side roads, the men all buried where they fell. Former slaves worked in the fields closer to the house. Only foodstuff was being grown. The stately trees once lining the drive to the front door were only stumps or splintered caricatures. It was a miracle the house remained in one piece.

He knocked on the door, Ann answered. Deprivation had bowed his sister-in-law's shoulders and left her gaunt, even her hair faded to gray. She spat in his face. He slipped his current letter under the door. Two days later Leo knocked on the door to the room Matt rented in a small hamlet about ten miles from home. Leo was twenty, face lined from the weight of his burdens. His eyes were bleak as he stared into Matt's eyes. The message was short and brutal.

"Father died at Gettysburg. Mother collapsed after we got word. She was dead a few months later. Ben could not come home because he would have been shot for spying. We got his last letter in '63. He was moving from one regiment to another as men were killed off. He must be dead. We don't know if he ever received the last packages we sent. The only thing keeping Ann on her feet is the children. Why in heaven would you think anyone here would wish to look upon your face?"

"I'm so sorry Leo, more than I can say. I'm sorry."

"Were you at Gettysburg killing our father or prancing around New York preaching your negroism? Was it a bullet from your gun killed him?"

"Don't you think I worried over that every minute? I wasn't the only one with family and friends on the other side. What else could we do but try to stay alive. I couldn't fight to keep people like cattle! Father branded people Leo. You don't treat a human being that way!"

"Who gives a damn about your conscience, you murdering swine. You raised your hand against your own. If you had not the courage to hold onto our birthright, you should have stayed run off like the coward you were. We would have been better off for it! God knows, I'd kill you now if I could."

Matt turned away from enraged features, so like his own. The young man's face was flushed and his eyes were flooded with unshed tears.

"Leo please..."

Matt turned back to an empty hallway. He reported back to his unit and performed his final duties immersed in the Indian conflict. Any remaining belief in justice was completely eradicated after seeing the new atrocities fed by fear, lust for gold and revenge on both sides. Like former slaves, some tribes took sides in the conflicts. It availed them nothing but broken treaties, starvation and incarceration. He could see the day when whole tribes no longer existed.

A clash with rebelling warriors garnered him a slashed face and a bullet creased skull. The doctors were amazed that there was no penetration or fracture, just an awful bloody gash and blindness. After months recuperating his sight slowly returned.

Matt mustered out, returning to New York, continued his studies and opened a law practice. He was working hard at making a new life. But drink smothered the pain during many nightmare ridden evenings. After spending one night drinking in a local tavern, he had been caught in the crossfire during some street brawl and new round of nightmare began. His precarious sanity was threatened more than anything previous on the horror ship.

Lost in memories, Matt sat beneath a pine, cushioned by the needles that carpeted the ground. Images rushed before his eyes and his head began to ache. Looking back he couldn't believe how naive he'd been. Freedom for the Negro was followed up with new sanctions against them. For many life was no different than before. And the Indians were losing ground every day to confinement and disease. Were his sympathies twisted in that regard as well? He had fought them regardless of his beliefs. How much sense did any of it make?

McNamara surprised him, coming in person to escort him out of San Francisco. Matt recalled his terror, the shame, of sitting in the carriage trembling as they went to the train station to begin his journey back to New York. Months later he sold McNamara his part of the business and left for the territories. Ignorant of life in the wild, he endured and came to appreciate the places away from civilization.

In all the years since he went his own way, shunning most company. More often than not an object of suspicion because he was not well off. He worked at whatever was at hand; mill rider, bronc buster and even plowed land for nestors in exchange for food when they allowed him. He had little pride left about such things. His occasional letters home were never answered. Of course they wouldn't be, but Matt continued to flog himself with that decision to continue writing in hope.

Reading his book always brought to mind Jimmy Stanwick. An uneducated street ruffian, Jimmy had shown him the badly spelled poetry he wrote. Matt made the mistake of taking an interest, helping the boy learn to read and write properly. Jimmy purchased a book of poetry with his first pay. But the day came when Jimmy lay screaming for his mother, bleeding in a muddy ditch with no aide to be had. Jimmy never knew who his mother was, but he using his last breaths begging her to save him before Matt put an end to his pain.

All those memories crashing around inside his skull, filled his head to bursting. He could feel the pressure building behind his eyes. The doctors swore the headaches were not caused by anything but his imagination. They performed thorough examinations of his skull for any abnormalities, as if palpating his head would tell them what was happening inside it. Matt was convinced the literal blinding pain would eventually put a permanent end to his sight. When it happened he would do for himself what he did for Jimmy that horrible day.

Right now he needed to take his laudanum and sleep. He never used it unless he got one of these bad ones, not wanting to wind up stealing to feed the addiction. So many of the men he fought with came away with horrible attachment to this concoction. Every time he was wounded, the fear of getting a permanent desire haunted him. It was bad enough he wound up drinking heavily after the war. Matt walked back, squeezing his eyes shut against the batches of sunlight breaking the heavy foliage. Even his spectacles weren't much help when the headache came on.

Sarah was sitting on the floor by her father's side when Matt stumbled into the cabin. His face was beaded with sweat. He was grimacing against the pain. She jumped to her feet alarmed by his appearance.

"Mr. Travers! What's wrong, what's happened?"

"Nothing, nothing. Headache real bad," he mumbled.

Matt tossed aside his bed roll and dug through his saddlebags until he found the little bottle secured in a small leather pouch and wrapped in cloth. His hands shook as he fumbled it loose from the bindings. Taking a deep breath he allowed only two drops of the tincture to fall on his tongue. He would sleep through the night and probably drag around the next day until the lassitude wore off, but anything was better than the ax blade slicing into his skull. He fumbled the bottle back into its wrappings and knotted the strings of the pouch tight. He would not forget to seal it away and keep it secured in his saddlebags.

A quick drink from his canteen washed the taste away. Intent on arranging his blankets, Matt was startled by Sarah standing over him.

"Mr. Travers, will you be alright?"

Matt couldn't hold back the flinch from the sound of her voice. Everything was so loud.

"Alright after I sleep. Honest lady I just need quiet awhile. Got shot...war...head hurts. Sleep please."

Sarah was still watching, worry escalating as Matt collapsed onto the blanket. He was shivering as if he were cold. She didn't know if it was the medicine he took or if he was feverish. He pulled his hat down over his eyes and curled up. She knelt down beside him to ease the second blanket over his shoulders. He curled up tighter and rocked himself. She backed away and stepped outside to warn Kevin that Mr. Travers was ill.

Kevin had insisted on scouting the area to insure their continued safety. She thought he was being overly paranoid. Mr. Travers opportunity for wrong doing was surely passed. Honestly, If Kevin was showing off for her, he was only causing her to rethink their possible engagement. Should he not be here at her side protecting them? A man needed common sense to survive in this country and the exasperating man didn't seem to have it right now.

Sarah paced back and forth for a while. She went back inside to fix an early supper. Mr. Travers never moved other than the occasional deep sighing breath. Sarah ate a solitary meal before resuming her pacing exercise before the cabin.

Finally Kevin stepped into the clearing. She ran over to him and hissed.

"Where have you been? I've been worried sick."

"Sarah, you wouldn't..."

"Shh...not so loud."

"What's wrong?"

"Come over here."

Sarah tugged him back toward the stand of pine.

"Where were you?"

"Like I was trying to tell you. I tried to follow Travers. I got lost."

Kevin flushed a deeper hue than usual as he showed her his lost puppy face.

"Lost!"

"Yeah, lost. I've been trying to get back here for more than an hour. He must have figured out I was following and laid a false trail. Why are we whispering?"

"Mr. Travers is inside."

"What, when did he do that?"

Sarah rolled her eyes and crossed her arms to keep from smacking Kevin.

"You have been gone half the day Kevin, not an hour! Mr. Travers appears to be very ill. If I understand him, he was wounded in the war. He took medicine and asked for quiet while he slept."

"Medicine, what kind of medicine?"

"That isn't any of our business Kevin. The man was in obvious pain. He's asleep. I don't think you could get him up if you tried. If you are so suspicious, why did you go off on this scouting trip through the woods and get lost? The man has done nothing to warrant anymore of these speculations. I made supper. Come in and eat. We are going to be on short rations until the boys get here. You can tell me about your scouting trip in the morning."

Sarah turned away, dismissing the entire matter. She was tired and now had double the worry. If Mr. Travers was down for another day, she would have to find his snares. Kevin never handled hunting on the ranch very well. Needless to say he was proving less than skilled for ranch life. Rabbit would not be on the menu at home for the coming year if she had anything to say about it.

"Wait a minute, Sarah. Look I'm sorry, alright? I'm trying to be, well you know. I'm sorry I worried you."

"I apologize if you think I was harsh Kevin. I'm just tired and anxious. That man saved my father's life, evidently at plenty of risk. We don't need to worry about anything but getting home. I don't expect you to have all the answers to this situation. But we can't go off the rails. Innocent til proven guilty remember?"

Kevin moved close and hugged Sarah. She was stiff in his arms then sighed and relaxed.

"Honey I've had a hard day and so have you. Let's just relax and try to enjoy the evening. The moons full tonight." He bent to kiss her. Sarah allowed his lips to lightly brush against hers before pulling away.

"Kevin I'm too tired and worried. How can you expect me to relax when you yourself remind me the stranger who saved father might still be a danger? Now both men are down. I've paced back and forth for hours worrying about you. I'm exhausted. I'm sure you you must be tired from your ordeal."

Sarah pulled away turning toward their shelter.

"Remember, keep it down Kevin," she

admonished just before she entered the cabin.

Kevin removed his hat to brush his hair back with his fingers. He pulled hard until his scalp tingled, then stalked in behind her. Sarah sat his plate on the table before settling down on her bedding. She pulled off her boots and lay down. She watched through narrowed eyes and raising ire as Kevin scraped his plate clean before shoving it away. He removed muddy boots, dropping them on the floor, the showy spurs clanging. He tossed them over his bedroll before stretching out on the floor beside her.

"Good night Sarah. I'm sure you'll feel alright in the morning sweetheart."

She twitched, but kissed him on the cheek and murmured 'good night'.

Kevin turned over a number of times, complete with grunts of dissatisfaction against sleeping another night on the floor. Exasperated, Sarah turned her face to the wall beneath her father's bunk. Tonight she absolutely would not spend any more time worrying about the current situation. Gil should be back in two days at most. Father would get well and Mr. Travers could have a job, which he seemed in sore need of. He didn't strike her as the 'reward hunting' type. But a job over the coming winter they could do. She did not know what to think about Kevin. He was entirely too inconsistent with his affections. I'll keep you safe one minute and off lost in the woods the next.

Bequiled and Bewildered

Sarah's anger kept her awake half the night. The sun's appearance found her stiff and more irritable than before. She lay there, surprised to see Mr. Travers sit up and stretch. He gazed around the room, blinked and smiled at her. He sighed and ran his fingers through snarled hair.

"Sorry about last night. I get real snappish when the pain comes."

"I understand. I didn't know how to help you. That frightened me."

"Didn't mean to scare you. Got shot during an Indian raid. Still pains me now and then."

"Oh, I understand. It's alright. I just wanted to help."

Matt got to his feet, swayed a moment and stretched once more.

"You couldn't do anything. I just have to sleep them off. I'll probably sleep most of the day too."

"Can you keep it down? I'm still trying to sleep," Kevin admonished from beneath his blankets.

"Sorry Harlan. I'm stepping out anyway."

Sarah watched Matt leave using the table and

the walls for support. He didn't look too steady at all. She checked her father's condition. He still seemed to be sleeping comfortably. She hoped he would awaken today. After folding her bedroll, Sarah left the cabin for a moment of privacy in the woods. She washed hands and face from her canteen before returning to see about breakfast. There were plenty of beans and cold rabbit. Mr. Travers had left the broth to stay hot over the fire. Sarah hoped her father would be able to eat it. She eventually divided the remnants between the three of them. After setting the filled plates on the table she rousted Kevin out.

Obviously unhappy, Kevin scrubbed at his face and sat down at the table. Sarah took her plate and settled in her place by the bunk. They were eating silently when Matt returned. His hair was wet and he appeared well scrubbed. His face was bare of spectacles for once. Sarah was surprised by the brightness of silvery gray eyes against his tanned complexion.

"Where did you find enough water to wash up?"

"Well actually I just wandered a different trail into the woods this morning and found this little seep along the mountain behind us."

"Please show me where. I'm dying for a

bathe."

Matt chuckled, rocking back on his heels. He braced himself on the table, took his plate and lowered himself carefully by the fireplace. He scraped some of the lukewarm beans into his mouth before saying more.

"There's not enough water trickling down from that hole for a bath Sarah."

Matt continued to chuckle as he focused on his food.

Sarah stared, rather bemused. He was handsome when he smiled.

"Well I'm going to move the horses to better grazing," Kevin said, pushing away from the table. He stepped over to Sarah and caught her chin between his fingers.

"You can show me the way to that water later on Sarah honey."

He pressed his lips to hers, tightening his fingers when she pulled back.

Matt got to his feet, leaving the partially eaten meal on the floor.

"I'll take the canteens to refill. Come on if you're going Miss Bethancourt."

He was out the door and into the trees before Sarah and Kevin parted. Kevin winked at Sarah before he left. Sarah ran in the general direction Matt took, her entreaties for him to wait disregarded. She was breathless and angry when she finally caught up with him. He was filling the canteens.

"You can wash up after I'm gone. I have to water the horses."

"It was Sarah a little while ago, Mr. Travers."

Matt felt his face grow hot. He stoppered the last canteen and turned to her.

"I meant no disrespect, mam." He tipped his hat in her direction and hurried away.

Sarah caught herself in time to prevent a righteous swear word from escaping. Men surely got on your last nerve. Growing up around cowhands tainted her vocabulary early. Her mother insisted on finishing school attempting to eradicate their influence. The results were dubious at best. Even now when Sarah was thwarted all the hands knew it. She could cuss a blue streak if her mother wasn't around. That a ragged saddle bum would dare treat her like that. The nerve of some people. Ignore her one minute and smile at her the next, then run off in the middle of her conversation.

Remembering her father, Sarah scrubbed as best she could and returned to the cabin. Matt was in front, currying that pitiful looking nag he rode. She stood in the doorway watching while taking apart her braid and attempting to comb out the tangles. Cobby tried to bite or kick his curry comb swinging tormentor every chance he got. It wasn't long, however, before Matt had him saddled and mounted up. Cobby was so battered, you wouldn't think he had the strength to buck like that. He sunfished like a dervish. Surely that wasn't helping Mr. Traver's headache!

"I'm going to ride out and check for sign. Whoever shot your father may have hold up like we did. Better be cautious. Won't be gone long."

"I'll be fine Mr. Travers. I am armed and Kevin is nearby." Sarah couldn't help her frosty tone. The man was staring.

Matt didn't say anything for another long moment. She wanted to retreat into the cabin when he abruptly departed without another word. What an insolent...

Sarah finally noticed Kevin was nowhere in sight of the cabin. She stomped inside and just missed putting her foot into Matt's plate. Mumbling under her breath she picked it up and sat it on the table rather forcefully. Serve him right if she served him the congealed beans for supper.

Matt rode along the narrow trail leading from

the cabin, noting the tracks the horses made while it was fairly muddy. He singled out Gil's cow pony and rode on eventually breaking through the brush onto the cliff side trail. On the surface Sarah Bethencourt was the kind of girl his family would not have approved of. He recognized the signs of finishing school manners. Yet her hands were work roughened proving she loved the outdoors and the responsibilities of ranching. The weird getup she was wearing would have given his mother a fit. He had not wanted to be caught staring, but for sure she was wearing pants underneath that short denim skirt. The clothes weren't fancy either, just a woolen shirt and plain leather vest. But that Spanish sombrero caught his attention. It had been resting against her back, like a picture frame for those copper curls come loose from her plait.

What she saw in that fickle, smooth talking Harlan he'd never understand. Goes to show education doesn't mean much if you don't use it. Harlan was a study in contradictions alright. Cocky one minute and helpless the next. Always blushing and wheedling when caught out in the open. Her father would disown...ah stop that thought, it brought too much pain. No, no one deserved that. If Miss Bethancourt married that tin plated, dime novel pretender, she would be back east in a hot minute with everything her father owned sold off for city life.

He continued his ride unable to shake the image of Sarah standing in the doorway with her copper sparked hair loose over her shoulders. Even after two nights in wrinkled clothes she was beautiful.

Cobby looked over his shoulder at the tormentor. The reins had gone slack and he refused to continue along the trail unless forced. There was nothing to eat on this rocky path increasing his ever present disgust with tormentors in general.

Beautiful. That's what Sarah was, beautiful. Matt looked around the mountains. He heard the hawk's cry and shading his eyes, searched the sky. It fell like a stone into the deep, brush strewn drop off alongside the trail. The screech of triumph echoed as the hawk suddenly rose into the air, prey dangling helpless from its talons.

Birds were to be envied, free to roam the skies, eat and rest at will. They lived, taught their offspring to fly and died. Matt was sure somewhere inside them it all made sense. They were, and that was all, no heartbreaking decisions just life without doubt. Being human was awaiting the next onslaught with trepidation. He remained on watch, until the hawk disappeared up the mountain. Suddenly, the wind picked up, causing Matt to hunch his shoulders against the sudden chill during the return trip.

Vexed Beyond Words!

William was confounded. Where was he? He felt too weak to call out for Frances Ann. For a moment he believed Sarah was singing softly to him. Why were they here? He left them both safe, at the ranch. Where was this place? He returned to darkness. The pounding ache couldn't follow him there.

Sarah choked back tears. She wouldn't give up hope. For a moment it appeared her father would awaken. His eyes opened, but he never focused on anything. He grunted in pain and blacked out again. It was a good sign wasn't it? She wished Gil would hurry. Once more she began to pace back and forth, agitation growing. Tears began to flow unrestrained.

Oh, the one thing she had not done since the night she left home was to pray. Standing there in the shadowed doorway she bowed her head, thanked God for sparing her father's life and for His help to get them safely home. A deep breath held and released signaled renewed determination. Sarah checked her sidearm and walked outside looking around for Kevin.

Her momentary lighter heart was replaced with irritation when she realized his horse was gone.

"I don't believe you're still trailing Matt around. Kevin Harlan you have to be the most hard headed man I've ever met!"

Where was he when she was supposedly in danger? Was he protecting her father? Standing guard anywhere? No he was riding around in territory he didn't know and would probably get lost, again! He might never find his way back at all. Really, this was all so ridiculous.

Kevin fumed while his pony picked its way through the thick brush. He had been watching that saddle bum real close. Contrary to what these cowboys believed, he wasn't a fool. The man had eyes for Sarah, oh yes he did. It wasn't going to happen, he'd make sure of that. Women were always taken in by penny dreadful, strong silent types, the unattainable ones. Where he came from all the silly girls thought cowboys were such heroes. They didn't see the reality; unwashed bodies, dung covered boots and chewing tobacco. Kevin wasn't going to remain here. He already invested too much time on this enterprise, but Sarah had been an unexpected bonus. She was stubborn as a mule alright enough. But when he did get a kiss, the feel of those womanly curves charged through him like lightening.

It would have been easy if the broken down bastard had stolen the money. Why hadn't he? Maybe he wasn't as down on his luck as it appeared. That Winchester was in mint condition, even he could see that. The man hadn't been wearing a sidearm when they got there, but after they settled in with him, it was soon hanging off his hip. It looked new too, not the battered relics most of the cowhands wore. He even slept with it on. Then Travers comes in claiming he's sick and Sarah went all soft hearted on him again. Didn't she know a man like that wouldn't want her pity? That girl was supposed to look all doe eyed at him, not some ragged wretched bastard! Oh, if only he knew what the man's game was. Why didn't the fool cut and run with that money? Why? He couldn't afford to have Sarah's head turned. There must be some way to make the man show his true intentions.

Damn it, all the stupid trees looked the same. Had he wandered off the trail? Travers should be just ahead of him. Sarah would be really angry if he got lost again. Kevin turned his mount around, unsure of his destination. Upset was the least of it now. His horse whinnied, causing him to jerk on the reins in surprise. A distant response gave him the general direction, but his mount moved off on its own. It was with no little relief the young man returned to the cabin, managing to elude the hard eyed young lady tapping her foot in the doorway.

He stalled his return indoors, reluctantly wiping down his pony. This is why cities had livery stables. Sarah would readjust to a life of refinement once they were away from here. The charming lady he met in Boston would once again come to the fore. No more camping trips, no snakes and slain carcasses hanging from trees. A carriage ride around the commons would certainly be more romantic than that filthy excursion, complete with unwashed cowhands and blood.

Out here, the hired help were too familiar with Sarah. The men praised her roping technique of all things, then scolded her when some chore was forgotten. What on earth was her father thinking allowing Sarah to herd cattle and rope steers? She even cleaned the stables and other disgusting activities. It also didn't help the fools thought his 'tenderfoot' status a source of hilarity. The jokes were stupid and insulting. Little did they realize he would have the last laugh. They would be looking for work and Boston would once again be his playground.

The Noose Tightens

Matt rode in with a stiff wind stirring up behind him. The temperature continued to fall. There would be more rain, or worse an early snowfall. He looked forward to none of it stuck in a cabin with a wounded man and his family. Cobby was side stepping and snorting every time the eddies stirred his mane. It didn't take him long to wipe the old horse down and leave him to snap at the wind between cropping the scant foilage. He had just reached out to open the door when it slammed open and Harlan stormed past him, red in the face and scowling. Matt tried to calm his racing heart and let go of his gun. He could have shot the young fool. The boy was absolutely oblivious to his surroundings. It could get him killed. Just the thought made Matt's temper rise. He stepped inside to find Sarah tight lipped and furious. He avoided her stare and raised chin by crouching before the fire and adding more fuel to it. The broth had boiled down, so he added more water.

"Kevin tried to follow you."

There was no follow up to the comment, so Matt turned to look at Sarah. The question was in the angle of his head. His eyes were obscured once more by his spectacles.

"He's suspicious of you and thinks you have other motives. He attempted to follow you, I should say. He got lost.

"I wasn't trying to hide where I was going. I would have been long gone and your father's body still on that ledge if I had wanted money. I have things I need to be seeing to and this has delayed me. Another storm maybe moving in on us and I..."

Matt stood up, suddenly speechless with rising anger and frustration. He directed a hard stare at Sarah and stalked out of the cabin. She was startled but took off after him. A fight with Kevin was not a good idea. Only there wasn't any confrontation. Matt once again disappeared into the forest. Sarah wondered how much more of this she could handle. Kevin was being an ass and Matt's abrupt departures and silence irritated her to no end. Fuming, Sarah realized her impotence in the situation. Perhaps the women clamoring for the right to vote and make decisions usually reserved for men had it right. All this bullheadedness was driving her around the bend.

Two hours later Sarah's mood took a lighter turn, when her father's eyes opened. She spoke softly to him, easing his agitated movements.

She rushed to spoon some of the broth into his mouth, elated when he appeared surprised and swallowed it. She sang to him until he appeared to fall asleep. He hadn't looked directly at her but the sound of her voice did seem to calm him. She was determined this was a good sign. Another hour passed without a sign of either of her errant protectors. At least she knew Matt was around, because his wall eyed mount snapped at her when she went to see if he was still there. She laughed in relief.

Matt returned to the cabin with the ever present rabbits dangling from his hand. There seemed to be an excessive amount of the creatures. Good in this situation, but Denver was beginning to look better and better for the winter. He called out to the occupants of the cabin before approaching the door. He had been away for some time and Harlan may have returned. If Harlan was suspicious of him, getting shot would be too likely. Matt shivered inside his coat and the rising wind actually pushed him through the door when Sarah called his name. She was alone. Where was that fool? If he got himself lost in the woods again, Matt wasn't going to go looking. Not even if Sarah asked. No absolutely not. With a grimace he hung the rabbits over the grate, took off his coat and built up the fire. It wasn't long before the meat was roasting. He had made it a point to avoid Sarah's gaze, unsettled by his attraction to her. He didn't need this, especially since that puppy was so determined to let Matt see he had a claim.

Sarah sat on her bedding watching Matt cook the meat. He dropped some greens into the broth and added more water to it. He never said a word or looked in her direction. The quiet made her uncomfortable, but if he was still angry about Kevin perhaps this once she would leave it be. Rain began to fall in a steady patter. Just as she thought to go call out for Kevin, he charged through the door, looking shocked when Matt's gun snapped up to cover him.

"Mr. Harlan, you should call out before you come in, considering the circumstances."

"...Uh...uh, you're right Matt. I wasn't thinking. Wasn't expecting the rain..."

Matt's stare was hard and accessing for a long moment. Then his gun slipped back into the holster on his hip. He turned back to the fire to watch over the food. Kevin kept one eye on the man has he went to his bedroll and sat down beside Sarah. She was obviously still angry at him. His smile didn't soften her this time.

She frowned and turned away, fussing with the blankets on her father's cot.

The remaining hours were tension filled as Kevin's attempts at conversation were not acknowledged. Sarah probably told Matt he was under suspicion. That would explain the gun when he walked in. The man hadn't been that guarded before. Damn, this would make things more difficult. They ate the wild greens and rabbit without comment and Matt cleaned up the area, all the while ignoring them.

"I, I forgot to mention, but my, my father woke up this afternoon."

Kevin twitched at her side, his face blank for a moment. Then he turned to her with his dazzling smile.

"Why that's fantastic Sarah, honey. Did he say anything? Any clue to who attacked him?"

"No, no he didn't speak at all. But he had a few sips of broth and then he went back to sleep."

Her expression was full of hope and lit up with her smile. Kevin took her into his arms and hugged her.

"Oh Sarah, that's great. See I told you he would pull through. It won't be long before we're home and this misadventure will be behind us."

"Thank you Kevin. I hope so I do."

She couldn't hold back her tears and Kevin pressed his wrinkled bandana into her hands.

Matt watched them interact, but said nothing. He acknowledged her information with a nod. She didn't know whether to be angry or not at his lack of verbal response. She returned Kevin's kerchief and tried to keep the frown from her face as he squeezed her hands a little too tight. Without any more comment, Sarah got into her bedding and tried to sleep.

Harlan and Matt didn't speak again until Kevin made ready for bed.

"Mr. Travers...uh Matt...look I'm sorry alright? I guess Sarah told you I was trying to follow you around today. I, I don't actually know what to say about that. I'm sorry to be, but well, I never felt for anyone before like I do Sarah and well, she, I mean I want her to see me as well..."

His speech trailed off into silence, his beseeching gaze directed at the blank features of the scarred cowboy. The silence held for a too long moment. A frown twisted Matt's features before he sighed heavily.

"This isn't the city Harlan. Things a man does tells more than what he says. I have business of my own. Once the old man is back with the cowhands you and your girl will be on your way, and I will be on mine. That will be the end of it."

Matt went to his bedroll and stretched out. He left Kevin staring at him in consternation. So this man was just going to ride away without reward of any kind? No money, not even a job?

Kevin rolled up in his own blankets listening to the annoying plonk, plonk plonk of water leaking from the ceiling. The old man had woken up, that could pose a serious problem. Sarah was real resistant to his attentions today. How could she stay mad for so long? He needed to think. What could he do about all this? His ruminations provided no answers and late into the night he dozed off.

The sun never broke through the clouds heavy with rain. Matt woke to gray shadows. He slept poorly during the night, disturbed by his continued confinement and the cannon shot thunder overhead. The room was damp and very chilled. Matt considered his options, but leaving a wounded man and a woman helpless didn't sit well. Tired of his indecision he dozed off, twitching now and then as the thunder continued to echo around the mountains.

It was just as dark when Matt woke again, but he rolled out shivering in the damp. After building up the fire, he broke his fast with a cup of the wild greens. Harlan woke, ignored him and staggered out into the rain. He came back wiping his face and hair down.

"Morning Travers."

"Harlan."

Kevin pulled a leg off the rabbit hanging over the fireplace, squatted by the fire and ate. No more was said. He occasionally glanced at Matt, but flushed and looked away if their eyes connected. Matt found this annoying, but was determined he wasn't going to get more involved with the irritating easterner than he already had. The chill in the air was increasing so the warmest place was directly before the fire. He may have to ride the trail and find the old man and his hands. It would be best if this rescue happened before they were trapped. Putting on coat, slicker and guns he left the cabin.

Cobby was in a real disagreeable mood and attempted to bite him more than once. Matt didn't win the stare down with his soggy mount this time. He had to admit his efforts were halfhearted. The idea of slipping and sliding down the mountain and ending over a cliff didn't sit well with him. He finally left Cobby and the other ponies beneath the overhang behind the cabin and hoped the storm passed quickly.

Sarah was awake when Matt returned. She was picking over a bit of meat, leaning against the cot. It was obvious she was avoiding any interaction with Harlan and himself. After removing his slicker and coat, Matt settled onto his blankets. Another blast of thunder startled the occupants. Matt sat, one hand clutching the blanket and the other his sidearm. The sounds of cannon continued to echo and vibrate the leaky timbers. He couldn't stop the minute twinges that gripped his muscles under the assault. He hoped no one noticed his trembling hands, when he took the short strips of leather and rope from his bag. Soon he was lost in the rhythm of weaving his Solomon knots. The low light didn't obstruct his efforts. His fingers knew the task even when his mind was lost to the battlefield.

Lightening, thunder and pounding rain curtailed any conversation. The trio sat, damp and sullen throughout the dreary day. Mr. Bethancourt roused once. He appeared to be attempting to sit up, but Sarah soothed him and managed to spoon some broth into his mouth. He was conscious enough to swallow, but the strength to speak seem to have eluded him. Realizing she wasn't a dream accounted for his agitation. He was a very protective man. His wife and daughter never left the ranch without him or Gil riding escort. Gradually exhaustion caught up with him and despite his desperate denials, he was asleep once more.

Bloodshed

Matt lay in his blankets listening to the water still leaking from the ceiling. The rain seemed to have stopped for now anyway. He was cold. Tossing the blankets aside, he lurched to his feet and stretched. It took a few minutes to ease cramped muscles which had stiffened attempting to protect him from each explosion of cannon. His sweat and the dampness made his clothes adhere to his skin. With a grimace, Matt made his way to the door and stepped outside. The sun was blazing as if the rain never happened, so he dug out his glasses and hooked them over his ears. Squinting against the glare from sun lite puddles, he went into the trees.

After taking a moment to wash up at the rivulet, he leaned against the stone breathing deeply. He was damned tired. They couldn't stay here and expect the old man to survive the deprivations. But to get him off this mountain seemed impossible. Harlan would be useless on the trail considering he couldn't read sign or handle a horse very well. Matt didn't know what to do about this. If there were bad men out there, they had to be long gone by now. Better to chance leaving than to do without supplies. Old Gil could have had an accident or met with foul play. They didn't know and seriously couldn't wait. Frustrated he wrestled with the pros and cons.

Sarah checked her father over for the hundredth time. Maybe they could build a travois to get him off the mountain. But further exposure to the weather would probably worsen his condition. She would ask Matt about it. Uncle Gil should have been back, but then the weather would have caused the men to take shelter if at all possible. Maybe they would get there today. Originally Uncle Gil planned for them to ride back to the base camp if they hadn't found sign of father. She thought their worries were almost over, if only he would ride in right now. Sighing, Sarah tucked her father in and stirred up the fire. After adding more wood, she stepped out to attend to her private needs.

The scent of wet pine invigorated her, despite the chilled air. She skipped over puddles and shivered when icy water slipped past the collar of her jacket. Water splashed off the rim of her sombrero. Unconsciously Sarah's spirit was lifted. She used her bandana to freshen up, dipping it a deep puddle of icy water. It was a momentary energy, however. Kevin's actions still irked her. When they got home, he would need to return to Boston. He was not functioning well in this crisis and she honestly couldn't see pursuing a relationship when he wasn't solid enough for this life.

Despite his talk of the city, Sarah could not see living the restricted life there. She hated every moment of her time spent at school. The first thing she had done when she returned home was saddle up her most rambunctious pony and ride as if the devil was after her, all over the range. She was stinking of sweat and half asleep from exhaustion when she got back. To her mother's consternation, she entered the house swearing loudly to never leave Colorado again, ever. She easily recalled her father's happy laughter when he wrapped her in one of his rib cracking bear hugs. Poor mother, she still didn't understand her wayward child.

The sun was warming her up as Sarah trekked back to the cabin. Her pleasant mood faded when she saw Kevin preparing to ride away from the cabin.

"Kevin! What on earth do you think you're doing?"

The pony spun on his heels, Kevin hauling on the reins. Something fell from the saddle into the mud. Furious, Sarah ran forward to give the idiot a piece of her mind. She was brought to a halt by the appearance of Kevin's sidearm aimed in her direction.

"Stop right there Sarah honey."

Kevin was holding a gun on her. She watched as he stepped down, watching her closely and groped around until he pulled her father's moneybelt from the mud. Spurred by outrage Sarah once more charged forward.

"How dare you! Have you lost your mind? You won't get away with this."

"Stop! Don't take another step. You wouldn't want me to shoot you now, would you?"

Kevin was standing tall, arm straight and gun steady in his hand.

"I was going to fight for you, honey. If those two tramps had done their job, I would have married you. You would have never known. But then I noticed some things. How eager you were to defend that saddle bum. How you didn't want my kisses anymore, always chasing after him. Did you lift that silly looking skirt for him this morning? Did you! It makes me mad. You want a broken down blind man over me! Oh yes, that's right, you don't know the tramp is going blind. Ha, ha look at Miss Bethencourt's face!"

Sarah was trembling with shock. What tramps? What was he talking about? This couldn't be happening. She forced herself to swallow, mouth dry and tongue cleaving to the roof of her mouth.

"Tell, tell me you didn't hurt father? Is, father..."

"Shut up, damn it. The old man didn't even wake up. He's dying anyway. Come to think of it those ranch hands are sure to be upset to find you dead out here with your old man. They might just hang that raggedy begger you're mooning over. Yeah, I like that idea."

"Kevin don't, don't do this."

"Kevin, don't do this," he simpered before pulling the trigger.

Sarah screamed, but it was Kevin's body folding over and falling to the ground. The shot seemed to repeat itself for an eternity to the woman's stunned senses. He said "I love you." He tried to kill her. Kevin's feet pounded the mud and one arm waved in the air scrabbling for purchase on nothing. Finally all movement ceased. Sarah continued to watch the body as if it was a rattler poised to strike. She didn't react when Matt moved passed her to kick Kevin's gun aside.

"See to your father girl. Now!"

Sarah shook all over and ran into the cabin. She hurried to lift her father back onto the cot.

His upper body was almost over the side. She was further shocked when he groaned and murmured her name. The bandages around his shoulder were displaced, faintly stained with new blood. She rushed to clean the wound and cover it over with a clean bandana from her bag. After making him comfortable, she held his hands tightly, so grateful they were both still alive.

Eventually Sarah spooned the remnants of the broth into his mouth. Her joy when he finished the cup and smiled, battled with her other reactions to events. There were episodes of panic when her breath would be lost, heart beating wildly. Then she would be fine again, if you discounted trembling hands and intermittent tears.

Faint Regret

A muscle twitched in Matt's jaw as he looked over the remains. Kevin's wallet was pretty flat. He wondered why the easterner didn't possess more than a comb and a creased, stained letter from Sarah dated a year ago. He laid them aside and turned the body over. The bullet entered just under Kevin's arm. Matt figured it broke bones then drilled his lungs and heart. There was blood in his gaping mouth, eyes wide, face flushed and swollen. He didn't die easy.

Matt knelt for a long time staring at the body. It could be Sarah's face with dead eyes and gaping mouth. He couldn't stop the gag reflex and heaved sour bile into the mud. After the army he swore never to kill another man. But he could not allow the girl to be killed. The writhing satisfaction in his gut was ruthlessly repressed. It wouldn't do to be happy the bastard was dead.

Before his thoughts got further lost considering motivations and guilt, Matt returned to the cabin and dug out his extra tin plate to dig a shallow grave. He hesitated when it came to the blankets. They may need Harlan's bedroll. No sense wasting them wrapping the body up. Sarah was sitting with her father, still teary eyed. There were no words he could think of to comfort her. He did check to see if her father was alright, quite surprised to find bloodshot eyes focused on him.

Standing around speechless wasn't going to accomplish anything. Squaring his shoulders, Matt went to bury the damned fool. It wasn't long before the repetitive effort to scour a trench in the damp soil settled his mind into the nothing which allowed him to face another day.

Sarah watched Matt come and go without a word. She busied herself putting the cabin in order. She went to the seep for more water, making an even thinner broth from the scant pieces of meat. Her father drank most of it. She told him what had been happening.

"I wish I could have warned you girl. I couldn't stop him. Two men tried to hold me up. I went for my gun. I don't, I don't remember anything after that."

"Oh, father! It sounds like Kevin sent those men after you. Did you know the men? Had you seen them before?"

"Worked on the ranch I think. Can't remember for sure," he whispered and closed his eyes.

"I don't understand why he would do such a thing? He was going to kill me and leave Matt to take the blame."

Sarah kissed her father's cheek, then pressed her ear to his chest just to hear his heart's rapid beating. They were alive! She was very grateful. Her prayer of thanks was interrupted by renewed tears. Exhaustion claimed her and she fell asleep. Will was not disturbed by his daughter's slumped form. They were not out of the woods yet. However, his frustration was not enough to overcome his wounded body's demand for rest. He slept.

Shadows pushed away the light inside the cabin as Sarah woke. She lit the fire and the lamp. She hadn't been sleeping very long, but her mind quickly turned to thoughts of Matt's well-being. He looked so sick when he came inside. It took more than a moment for her to realize the plate was being used to bury Kevin. They would be dead for certain if not for him. There could be no effort spared to make him see how grateful they were.

Her father moved restlessly until she sooth his anxiety with her presence. She kissed him on the cheek.

"Tell me about this man. The one I saw before. You say he found me?"

"He went out to bury Kevin. I'm worried father. He looked ill. I thought he might faint away. He said he brought you off a ledge and found this cabin, patched you up. Oh he was so protective. We had to prove who we were before he lowered his rifle. Even then he kept us under the gun. He never touched the money! It was lying right next to you and the latches hadn't been touched! Who would resist such a temptation? Even Uncle Gil was surprised."

"Well, I owe him. I owe him big and I'll see to it Sarah don't worry none."

"Dad, you know you always told me never settle for less than a man I could respect. Well, Matt is...he is. I think I found him." Her eyes filled with tears again at her declaration.

"Sarah," her father groaned and shook his head, "you were nearly engaged to that idiot easterner and he was no good. Don't start talking about any more fiancés, I won't live through another one, I won't."

"Oh dad I..." Sarah had the grace to blush red and covered her hot cheeks. "Get some sleep. Gil should be back today. We can go home."

"I can't wait," he mumbled. "Wake me when he gets here."

Sarah smiled and pulled the blankets to his neck tucking him in. She stepped out of the room, breathing deeply of the mountain air. They were alive, thank God. Matt was here and they were safe. As she thought of him Matt stepped around the corner of the cabin.

"I unsaddled his horse. Come morning we get going whether Gil is back or not."

"Yes, I think so too. Dad's able to talk now. The men who tried to rob my father were former hands."

Matt frowned at that.

"Lucky for him they made due with his horse and rig instead of going for the money. But we don't have enough ammunition to hold them off if they do show up again. Harlan claimed to be following me around, but there's no way to know what he was doing out here."

"Well, anything, anything at all you have it. I, we we're grateful Matt."

Sarah managed to look up into his eyes. She levered up and kissed his cheek.

Matt stepped away and frowned at her.

"Get inside and see to your father," he snapped.

Her eyes filled with tears again, but that didn't soften Matt. He turned away and disappeared into the trees, again. After the shocks of the day, this obvious rejection brought a fresh round of tears.

Matt could hear her sobbing, so he walked

faster.

Sarah didn't know how long she stood clutching the door frame and crying. It was so humiliating. He probably thought she was the most spoiled, fickle and callous woman alive. Dad was right, she didn't know her own mind and she was courting disaster once again. Obviously Matt found nothing attractive about a girl who could kiss him after he'd killed her near fiancé. Sarah's face flamed in shame again. She went inside and shut the door firmly behind her.

Matt held his head under the trickle of water using his bandana to scrub the worst of the filth from his body. It was cold, but he was sure there was still blood mixed with the mud on his hands. He gagged and retched for a long time. His chest and stomach burned when he managed to stagger back to the water. He rinsed his mouth and washed again. Alone, no one could witness his weakness. He cried, an awkward process that did not ease his disgust. If he hadn't killed Harlan two people might have died. He could have been digging Sarah's grave. He shivered continuously as he dressed and shrugged into his coat. He had no choice to go back and snub that girl. It was a kiss on the cheek, didn't mean anything but he, he didn't dare think. He was broken and no good would come of it.

Sarah was there looking vulnerable and frightened of him as he walked in.

"Miss Bethencourt, I apologize for my rough manner. I was out of line."

"I owe you the apology, Mr. Travers. I am not normally so ill-mannered and, and forward. I can only think the stress of the day... I ask your pardon."

Sarah stood by the fireplace wringing her hands as she spoke to him. Matt was watching the firelight glinting in her hair. She began to fumble at her skirt in confusion at his distraction. He finally tore his eyes away from her.

"I didn't mean to speak so harsh to you Sarah. I don't like killing a man."

He sighed.

"I'm tired girl. The ground was, ah I'm sorry. We better turn in. I'm too tired."

All he had to do was cross the room to his bedroll. It seemed a long way off.

"You haven't eaten. I..."

"I couldn't." The thought made him nauseous again.

"Some coffee?"

"No, no nothing. Just get to sleep."

He avoided her by walking to the other side of

the table and kneeling beside his bedding.

She followed him and the muscles in his shoulders tightened at her hovering.

"I hope Kev...he didn't take anything."

"Take? What?"

"He said, he said he went through your things."

Matt spun on his heels and jumped to his feet.

"That bastard, I.."

Sarah and backed away, shocked by his reaction. Suddenly Matt's face was bleached of all color and he swayed as if struck. Sarah rushed forward and wrapped her arms around his waist.

"Matt, Matt what is it?" She staggered as his weight shifted again.

"Here sit, no no in the chair."

Matt fell into it and covered his face with unsteady hands.

Sarah ran to Kevin's saddlebags and dumped the contents on the floor. Her own hands shook as she found his silver plated flask and rushed to splash the brandy into a cup.

"Here drink this, drink it!"

She pushed his hands away from his face and pushed the cup to his lips.

"Drink it down!"

Matt grimaced at the taste but took the cup

and drained it. Sarah watched him. He never looked up, but after awhile his color returned and his breathing slowed. The silence stretched.

She sighed. An owl hooted and swooped over the roof. One of the horses bumped the wall and snorted. Probably his.

"I better check around outside." Matt's voice startled her from where ever her numb mind had gone. Before she could say a word he was up and out the door.

He was gone so long she got nervous and placed her gun on the table.

Finally he stepped back inside.

"Thank God." He looked surprised at her relief.

"Everything's alright. No signs of anyone around."

"Good. Would you sit down here for a minute Matt?"

He folded his arms and backed away from her.

"It's late Sarah. We need to sleep."

"You need to sit and hear what I have to say," she snapped. She surprised him again.

He approached the chair as if she was a threat and sat down.

Sarah took a deep breath.

"You have suffered more than inconvenience

because you stopped to help my father. I'm sorry Kevin went through your belongs, but Matt, what he told me doesn't make any difference. I mean..."

"What did he say?"

"He...your eyes, that the doctors didn't know how long your sight might last."

Her voice was a whisper that screamed to him of pity. He clenched his fists in an effort to keep still and not scare her to death. If Harlan was alive right now, he would probably have killed him for this.

"...and I think you are just the bravest man I'ver ever met. Twice you have risked everything for strangers and I, I just wanted you to know..."

Suddenly she was on her feet and around the table. Before he could move her arms encircled his shoulders and she hugged him hard as she could. Matt wanted to get away but they were a vise stealing his breath and the strength from his body. Then his arms came up and wrapped around her waist. He was hugging her back. He turned his face away from the firelight into the soft darkness of her body. His throat ached and when he would have pulled away, her arms tightened. She laid her cheek against the tangled curls on his head and murmured, "It's alright", over and over again.

On the cot in the corner William Bethencourt

listened as well as watched his daughter's grieving face. Sarah never could resist a wounded critter and it looked as if she really lost her heart to this one. The easterner never made her look so broken hearted even when he betrayed her and died.

Matt could not remember being so tired when he finally rolled up in his blankets. Across the room Sarah smiled and his heart beat faster. He smiled back then quickly covered his face with his hat.

Resolutions

Come morning, Matt found Mr. Bethancourt awake. He nodded at the young man so Matt went over to check his wounds. He helped him sit up in the bunk and drink some water.

"I intend to pack us out of here today. No sense waiting on your foreman. Something could have happened to him."

"Gil's an experienced hand in these mountains. But you're right anything is possible. I think it would be better if you rode down and brought the men back. Sarah says the camp was completely outfitted to look for me as long as it took. We could hold up here till I was better if they set up camp. Some of them could go on back and let my wife know we're okay. That trail is barely passable during wet weather. Gil and the boys might be trying to break a new trail to get here if there's been a landslide or something. If you can't get through turn back and we will manage, cause I know they won't stop till they make it. Try to shoot something other than rabbit and we'll be set."

Will tried for a steely eyed glare, but he must have looked the fool because Sarah's giggle surprised both the men.

Matt scratched his head and frowned.

"I don't like it."

"Neither do I but..."

"We may not have a choice." Sarah chimed in. She was sitting up in her blankets yawning and stretching. "Matt can check his rabbit snares and that should tied us over."

Will grunted.

"When we get home I'm telling Freida no more Hassenpfeffer. Don't care what she thinks we'll get another cook if we have to."

Sarah laughed. Freida was more likely to toss her father off the ranch than quite her job. Both her sons had worked the ranch and now had their own homesteads and families.

"A man's got a right to a decent meal. I don't know what you were thinking girl, but you are going back to the kitchen!"

Sarah's mouth fell open in outrage.

"No, no Mr. Bethencourt Sarah didn't cook the stew. That was me!"

"You tryin' to poison me boy?" Will peered at Matt through narrowed eyes.

In spite of his embarrassment Matt joined Sarah in laughter. Well, more like a big smile for Matt who rarely found reason to laugh out loud. Will's effort to hang on to his ire made Sarah laugh harder. It was some time before the raucous sounds faded.

Sarah finally strapped on her gun and excused herself. She returned to the cabin washed up and braided her hair. Matt watched her from the corner of his eye during that process. Once she caught his gaze and smiled.

He loved her.

He sat on his bedroll cleaning and reloading their guns, his stomach growling from hunger.

He loved her.

Sarah noticed Matt was working really hard. The rag flew back and forth across his rifle as if it could shine brighter. When he finished he went off to check his snares, disappointed but not surprised to find them empty. The rain would have kept anything in the vicinity under cover.

"Stay close to the cabin. Keep your guns near at hand."

Will slipped his hand gun beneath his blankets.

"I'm still not sure about this Mr. Bethancourt."

"Well son, it's you or Sarah and I think she's safer here. Trying to get me off this mountain may kill us all. Besides I ain't eating any more rabbit. So ride out boy and be careful."

Matt shook Will's hand before hoisting

his saddle to his shoulder. He left the cabin to do battle with Cobby. Sarah watched from the doorway, rifle in hand, while Matt saddled then went through the murderously intent exercise Cobby took to unseat him. When she judged it safe she stepped out to wish him well.

"Stay close Sarah. I'll be fast as I can."

"Don't worry about us. Watch the trail and take care."

With a nod Matt was gone. Sarah watched until she lost sight of him and returned to the cabin. Will was dozing when she got inside, so she freshened up the coffee, fretted over what she could scrap together for her father. She was sipping on the bitter liquid when shots were clearly heard. She paid no attention to the coffee splashing into the flames as he tossed the cup away in surprise.

She ran to her father's side as he struggled to push himself upright.

"Sarah, we got to stay together. You can't go out there after him. They might be waiting for just that."

"No dad, Matt..."

"I know Sarah, but he may have got them. If he didn't we still have to wait."

Sarah couldn't keep away from the window,

however. She slid along the wall and tried to peek out for any sign of Matt. Her heart was beating so quick she was finding it hard to breath.

Endless minutes passed with no indication of what had happened out there, then suddenly she could see Matt's pony. Sarah sprang for the door, ignoring Will's weak sound of protest. If someone shot her now so be it, she could not leave Matt slumped there. Cobby stood just beneath the shadow of the trees at the edge of the clearing. She slowed to a walk and spoke softly as she called to Matt.

"Matt, Matt it's Sarah. Can you hear me? Matt can you..."

"The old man, oh damn Sarah the old man...," he gasped. She barely took in his words at the sight of the ragged hole in his coat.

Then he passed out and his pony snorted and shied away from her. She wasn't a fool to approach a spooked animal especially one as nasty tempered as Matt's.

"I just want to help him Cobby. Let me get Matt down," she continued to cajole and took another step. He bared his teeth and she stopped. The old man? No, no Uncle Gil would never! But what other old man could it be. Oh God, what if? The idea rocked Sarah's world completely off it's axis.

"Matt, Matt please you have to get off. I can't get to you. Please Matt wake up!"

A groan heralded Matt's return to consciousness.

"Matt get down."

"Sarah I, right. Down." And he slid from the saddle. Cobby snapped at the air and danced away from the body. She rushed to help him up, but he was dead weight.

"Sa-rah no, Will save Will. The old man after him," he gasped.

Matt grabbed her roughly with his good arm and shook her though he nearly passed out again. Gritting his teeth against the urge to vomit, he swore.

"Damn girl, your fa..." His face twisted horribly and he couldn't stop his body shutting down.

Sarah understood, she did. Though she was frantic for Matt she ran back to the cabin wondering why she was still alive if Gil had betrayed them. Did he think Matt was dead? Would he come here? Could her father kill him, could she? Was he watching? Did he think Matt was dead? There was no way he could have got to her father when she was right there.

Even so she was startled to see the door open. Gripping her sidearm, Sarah crept on and peeked in. Gil was holding a gun on her dad.

"Get in here Sarah honey. You won't be shooting me cause Will will take a bullet before I drop."

Gil was standing on the other side of the table away from the fireplace, his gun hand steady as always. Her father was propped up in bed as she left him. His face was pale and sweating. Their eyes must be the same, stunned by impossibility of this moment.

"This ain't no standoff Will. I'll shoot ya, no doubt."

"Why Gil? I don't understand? You and Harlan?"

"Why! You're sayin' you don't know why? I broke my back for you. Helped you make a fortune and what did I git? How many broken bones, freezing nights savin' your cattle, fightin' off rustlers. You name it I did it. Worked my tail off for you Will. What did I git?! And then this half breed lookin' devil comes along and saves your hide. You always had too much damn luck. And then he kills my son!"

Both Will and Sarah shouted in surprised denial.

"No Gil, tell me it ain't so. Harlan was your son? Why didn't you tell me? The boy..."

"You think when I found out I wanted him breakin' his back for a dollar a day? I spent all I had to make sure that woman took him back east to educate him for something better. We would have had it all and no one the wiser. Kevin was to marry her."

"Gil you know I would have helped you, you know that!"

Will couldn't believe what he was hearing. Harlan could have grown up on the ranch and gone back east to finish schooling like Sarah. They could have been brought up together, instead.

"Harlan wanted to kill Sarah, Gil. He wanted to kill her!"

Gil fingered the trigger guard back and that snapped Sarah out of her shock. She stepped forward. He ignored the gun in her hands, so sure affection would hamper her intent.

"Uncle Gil. I can't let you hurt dad."

He never took his eyes off Will.

"This is between me and your pa, Sarah. I'll get to you soon enough."

Surely her heart stopped at the cold resolution

in that statement. This man had held her in his arms, rocked her to sleep many a night and taught her how to ranch and survive the rough life they led. How could he have hated them so much?

"I offered you part of my own ranch Gil. You could have made a home for your boy right here."

Will was praying Sarah would survive this. Gil didn't know about his gun, but the man was a good shot and he had Will dead to rights. They might both eat lead today.

"What the hell would I want with the ridge line. The grazing over there ain't half as good as you got. You think I would a been satisfied with your leavings? Stake me with cattle you don't want? When ya went into business with them miners, ya didn't offer any of that!"

"You know I loaned them money when they had none. No one knew they would make a big strike. You told me yourself you thought I was throwing money away after dreamers. Remember it how it was Gil. You had your chances just like everyone else out here. If you were too scared to take the risks it ain't my fault!"

Gil flushed, enraged at the accusations. He glared at Sarah, daring her to shoot.

"Kevin wasn't much, but he was my flesh and blood. I seen you coolin' to him the last few weeks. I knew you was gonna change your mind. We decided to go for the money, only Kevin hired on those two lay abouts to do the deed and botch the damn job! But it's my time now."

Sarah's chin lifted. Nobody was hurting her dad today.

"No Sarah!"

Distracted by Will's shout, Gil's shot went wide and smashed into the wall.

Will's gun discharged at the same time, burned through the blankets and struck Gil in the lower abdomen. Sarah's bullet smacked into his body just below his sternum. Desperate to stop him, she pulled the trigger again. Her father's shouting stopped her before she emptied her gun.

The air was thick with gun powder. Gil lay face up in the lamp light. Red stains spread across his shirt front. Sarah walked over to the body and stared for a moment. She bent on shaky knees, removed the gun from Gil's hand and backed away. She managed to look at her father and realized he was still alive. She just walked over and sat on the bunk taking his trembling hand in hers.

Sarah looked around the room. Matt's book lay on the table top where he left it before riding out. Her father's shout of surprise went unheeded as she rushed outside with a canteen, burning with fear that Matt had died because she was in shock. Cobby stood nearby suspicious eyes locked on his downed master. His ears pricked forward at her approach, but he didn't charge or snap. Quickly Sarah checked Matt over. His heart was still beating. She wiped his face and begged him to wake up, so she could get him inside.

Still she was frightened when his eyelids fluttered open and there was a moment when he didn't recognized her or remember what had happened. She could see the confusion.

"It's alright now Matt. We stopped him. Gil's dead. It's alright."

He attempted to speak but didn't have the energy. She got him to take a few sips of water before she struggle to get him standing. It was a long difficult journey back to the cabin. He passed out once again, so she ran inside to get bandages to stop the bleeding as best she could. Maybe another hour went by before she managed to get him inside, then lowered him to his blankets she had laid out.

Her father lay quiet while she tended Matt. The bullet was still in his shoulder. It needed out but her hands were just too unsteady to do the deed at the moment.

"Sa-rah, thought he killed you, Sarah. Thought...glad glad you're not..."

"No Matt, father and I are both fine. Gil's dead. We...we both." She didn't try to hold back her tears. She still had to get Gil's body out of the cabin. None of them could sleep with his body there.

"Medicine, in my bag. Just a drop or two please, hurts Sarah." Matt choked back the urge to throw up. The pain was bringing back the memories of war and the ship.

"Yes, I remember. Just hold on Matt I'll take care of you. Don't worry."

It didn't take long to find the little bag with the tiny bottle in it. He was grateful for the dulling of his senses.

"Sarah, no more. No more even if I ask, promise," he whispered.

She frowned, but nodded agreement and Matt finally relaxed on the blankets.

"Sorry can't help, sorry."

She waited until he appeared to sleep, although there was a grimace now and then. First light she had to get that bullet out. This was all too much, but she wasn't done.

Despite her father's protest, Sarah managed to move Gil's body out of cabin. There was no way she could do anything else, so she left him there. She went back inside, barred the door and went to her blankets. Completely spent, Sarah laid down and slept. Her father lay much longer watching the two young people sleep. He would probably never be able to tell how proud of her he was. Sarah was one to ride the river with, no doubt about it.

The Ties that Bind

Frances Ann Bethancourt paced the length of the porch shading her eyes from the noonday sun. Her daughter and the hands had gone looking for William nearly two weeks ago. First she worried, then she was terrified. For the past two days she had not slept or eaten. This morning she put on her dark gray Sunday dress and coiled her graying auburn hair tightly at the nap of her neck. The nights were very cold, the more so since William was not there to hold her. He was hurt on the trail or worse robbed of the money he carried, otherwise everyone would be back. She would rather be fussing over her stubborn man by now.

The door opened behind her and Frieda stepped out. The cook watched Frances pace before shaking her head in frustration. She sat down in one of the rocking chairs. Everyday Frances had put on her prettiest dresses. This was a bad sign, this drab church going dress. Frieda sipped her coffee in silence. Frances' thin form moved back and forth, the numerous petticoats sweeping the porch. Her hands were twisting and knotting her handkerchief.

Both women lept to their feet when one of the stable hands came running from the barn.

"Their back, the boys are back. I could see Miss Sarah's sombrero from the loft."

He was pointing in the barn's direction which blocked the women's view of the distant mountains and narrow tree shrouded trails.

"Ya can't see 'em now Freddy. Almost to the house though."

The man ran back to the barn to make ready for the influx of exhausted horses. Men began to rush back and forth. Frieda put her arm around the frail bodied woman and held on.

"Oh Freddie what if..."

"None of that nonsense, you hear me. William is one strong mule headed man. He probably fell on his head and they had to tie him to the saddle!"

Frances laughed but it turned into a sob and she wept onto Frieda's shoulder. It was past time for the tears to fall. Now what ever had to be done, no matter how bad it was Frances would present a strong face by the time the party arrived. It was the longest two hours of their lives. Both considered the worst as the solemn group arrived.

Frances almost fainted when she realized William was mounted, but looking as if he wished he was not. Sarah smiled when she saw her mother and Frieda rush down the steps.

It was the cook who noticed the man strapped

to a travois. Frieda had the men bring him into the quest room they kept aside for anyone seriously ill. She wondered where Gil was and that lazy easterner who had come to visit. Maybe the foreman had finally taken him to task. But that would be explained later, this young man needed tending bad and she sat to clean his wound and give him a thorough scrubbing.

When Sarah came in to help, Frieda took one look at her pinched wan face and chased her off to bed. For once William argued not at all to a hot bath and a long sleep beside his exhausted wife.

One of the hands was riding to see if the doctor was still at Wimbly's. Soon everything would be set right.

Breakin' A New Trail

Matt blinked, then turned his head away from the light. He attempted to go back to the quiet cocoon, but the banging of a tin pan snatched him into complete awareness. A moment more and it occurred to him he was resting on a real bed with flannel sheets and goose down pillows. A breeze stirred his hair, so he turned to see an open window. Curtains with a rose pattern lifted in the air. Voices drifted to him, talk of fences and stock, chores to be done.

He moved, becoming aware of bandages swathing his chest and tying his left arm down. He experimented, moving parts of his body until he was sure all of him was there. He tried to remember how he got to this place, however fell asleep during the effort.

Matt's eyes opened again just as Sarah stepped through the bedroom door. Her face lit with joy at the sight of him?

"Matt, you're awake!"

He watched in amazement as the girl with copper hair crossed the room and planted a long kiss on his lips. She smelled like magnolia blossoms. Surely this was a dream.

Please, please let him stay here.

Sarah laid her beautiful head very gently on his good shoulder.

Matt realized he was delirious and didn't care at all. He inhaled deep as he could without pain to hold her essence inside.

"Sarah? Are you, is this real?" It's a wonder she heard the broken whisper, his throat was bone dry from fever and weakness.

"Oh yes, Matt. It's real."

"Where?"

"Home, Matt," she raised her head and gazed into his tired eyes. "We are home, understand?"

He sighed, content to let his eyes feast on her face for the moment. He would rest again and she would still be there.

"Yes," she whispered as if answering his unspoken thought. He didn't mind dreaming Sarah kissed him, even if his lips were cracked and sore.

Sarah listened to his heart's steady beat sooth her to sleep.

PATRICIA I. WILLIAMS

ABOUT THE AUTHOR

Born in New Orleans, La. and lived in Alexandria until she was twelve, Patricia I. Williams fell in love with Southern California on arrival. She would not want to live anywhere else, at least for this lifetime. She loves knowing the ocean is just beyond the hill and that Disneyland is the happiest place on earth. She enjoys traveling through the Southwest. The history and legends fuel a lot of imaginative Wild West adventures. She loves Science Fiction, film and books. Believes horses, dogs and cats are ideal companions.

Her faith in Jehovah keeps her grounded. She believes one lifetime is not long enough to learn everything. She is wary of all information because it most often is dependent on the good intentions of the provider. These days she finds pleasure is seeing her grandchildren's curiosity about the world around them.